FACE OF THE SUN

THE FRONTIER
BOOK 1

LEROY A. PETERS

This book is dedicated to my cousin Nathan Peters Jr. You are the closest thing to an older brother that I will ever have.

-Love,
LeRoy

FOREWORD

Lazarus Buchanan was a trapper's trapper. A man's man. If he was your friend then you had a friend for life, but if he was your enemy, then may God have mercy on your soul. Respected by the tribes, both friend and foe, Lazarus was no run-of-the-mill mountain man. Years of trapping, hunting, and living in the Northern Rockies, hardened him and made his senses acute, which have served him well as one of the most successful and legendary mountain men. This is his story.

INTRODUCTION

~

May of 1822, near Silver Bow Creek, Montana.

Lazarus Buchanan sat cleaning his Harper's Ferry rifle. It was one of two rifles that he personally owned. The other was a Pennsylvania rifle, also known as the Kentucky long rifle. He, and his nine year old son Amos, just returned from a hunt earlier that morning. He made it a habit of checking and cleaning his weapons before and after a hunt as he sat outside the cabin, he shared with his two wives who were gutting and cleaning the elk that he and their son just brought in. Dark Wind, who was Flathead Indian, was Amos's mother and had been happily married to Lazarus for eleven years. Mountain Flower was Nez Perce Indian and mother of Lazarus's three-year-old twin sons Nicodemus and Joseph and had been married to Lazarus for ten years. The trapper paused for a minute as he watched his wives and mothers of his children work on the elk carcass. Most of the meat will be hung in the smokehouse that he and his uncle built along with the cabin that he now shared with them. Uncle Amos. Lazarus thought about him a lot. He met his demise at the hands of a Blackfoot lance nine years ago, just a few months after young Amos was born. Lazarus owed a lot to his maternal uncle. It was he who brought his nephew out west to become a trapper and mountain man twelve years ago when Lazarus was just sixteen. Now twenty-eight and an experienced mountain man, Lazarus took the lessons taught to him by his beloved uncle about the ways of the frontier. These lessons not only helped Lazarus to survive but also showed him something else: true grit. Even though there were no guarantees that a man would survive the frontier with all its dangers, from unpredictable weather to wild animals, such as the dreaded grizzly bear, hostile Indians like the Blackfeet, and even other trappers who would rob you and slit your throat in the process. Lazarus knew tougher men who had either quit the mountains, like John Colter, because he could no longer deal with the dangers, or men who had succumbed to it, like his Uncle Amos.

With summer around the corner, it would be time to travel to St. Louis. Lazarus and his family often did that in summer to sell their plews and resupply for the next two trapping seasons. He often thought about his life over the past twelve years and how far he had come. Wow! "Has it been twelve years already," he thought to himself. "I remember it as if it was yesterday." He went to check his son's rifle to see if he cleaned it thoroughly while memories flowed through his head.

1

THE VISITOR

LAZARUS JOHN BUCHANAN was born on New Year's Day, January 1, 1794, in Dover, Delaware. He was the third of four children and the youngest son of Peter and Lydia Buchanan. His parents were Scottish immigrants from the Highlands of Scotland, from the town of Inveraray. Peter Buchanan was a successful shoemaker or cordwainer, while Lydia's father Angus Mackinnon was a professional boxer, who traveled up and down Great Britain, making his living as a fighter.

Angus Mackinnon was a giant, at 6 feet, 10 inches tall, and weighed over 300 pounds, he was surprisingly agile for a man his size. He won more fights than he lost and was careful with his money, unlike most fighters like him. He retired from boxing and settled in Inveraray with his wife Murron and their two children Lydia and Amos.

When Peter decided to uproot the family from Scotland to America, Angus, now a widower of three months decided to accompany his daughter and her family. He wasn't alone. Amos who was still a teenager and close to his father, decided that there was nothing left in Scotland for him either, since his mother's passing. Peter thought it was an excellent idea to have his father and brother-in-law come with the family to start a new life in America, since they were already close to his sons Peter Jr. and Paul.

Not long after settling in the state capital of Dover, Peter Buchanan, immediately set up shop and started his cordwainer business. One year later, Lydia would have Lazarus, who would be the first member of their family from either side to be born in America. Now while Lydia was brunette, as was her husband, and late mother, both her father and brother had sandy white hair.

Out of all the four Buchanan children, Lazarus would inherit his maternal grandfather's genes. Not just having white sandy hair, but by the time he was sixteen years old, he was already tall at six feet, six inches, and weighing two hundred and sixty pounds. Angus Mackinnon loved being a grandfather and doted on his grandchildren, more so than his daughter and son-in-law.

When Peter and Lydia welcomed their only daughter Leah in the spring of 1796, to say that the retired Scottish boxer was overjoyed would be an understatement. Amos Mackinnon was just fourteen years older than his nephew Lazarus. Like his father, he doted on his nephews and now niece and tried to set a good example for them. But he was restless and never really felt accepted in the community, mainly because of his Scottish accent and background. In 1798, when Lazarus was four, Amos joined the army, much to the chagrin of his sister. It would be over ten years before the family would see him again.

"Expelled!?" shouted Peter Buchanan.

It was the middle of January 1810. Lazarus had just turned sixteen, but this was not a celebration. "How do you get expelled at the beginning of the semester?"

"He was fighting again," said Lydia.

Lazarus was standing in the middle of the kitchen, with his head bowed. His parents both looked like they were about to pop a blood vessel. His grandfather Angus, just sat quietly listening.

"This is the fourth time you have gotten in trouble for fighting Lazarus," shouted Lydia in her thick Scottish brogue. "What do you have to say for yourself?"

"He had it coming," Lazarus answered.

"Don't you get smart with your mum," said Peter Buchanan. "Or I swear I will pup ya!"

"Take it easy Peter," said Angus.

Ever since the boy and his older brothers started walking, their grandfather taught them how to fight and never back down from bullies, despite their parent's reservations. While Peter Jr. and Paul were even-tempered men and were not above finding ways to avoid a fight, Lazarus was hot-tempered and while he didn't go looking for trouble, he never backed down from it, especially if that trouble was coming from Marcus Rhodes.

"Tell me," said Grandpa Angus. "Is that Marcus Rhodes going to be expelled?"

"It doesn't matter Da," said Lydia.

"It does if he is the one who started the fight," said Grandpa Angus. "That spoiled rich brat has made Lazarus's life a living hell, ever since you two enrolled him in that uppity private school for the rich elite's spoiled brats."

"You are not helping the situation Da," said Lydia.

"Besides, that is not the only reason he was expelled," added Peter.

Grandpa Angus had a look of confusion on his face.

"Poor Ms. Howard will be lucky if she can ever see out of her right eye again," said Peter.

"You hit your teacher?" exclaimed Grandpa Angus.

"It was an accident Grand Da," said Lazarus.

"Just how do you accidentally hit your teacher?" asked Lydia.

Lazarus just shrugged. "She got in the way I guess."

Angus Mackinnon guffawed. Not wanting to face his wife's wrath, Peter Buchanan managed to stifle a chuckle. "You think this is amusing Da?" asked Lydia.

"A little bit."

At that moment there was a knock on the front door. Fourteen-year-old Leah Buchanan, went to answer it and was greeted by her two eldest brothers twenty-one-year-old Peter Buchanan Jr and twenty-year-old Paul Buchanan. Peter Jr. had followed his father's footsteps into the cordwainer business, while Paul had gotten married last summer to a farmer's daughter and became a farmer himself. The two men, guided by their baby sister, entered their parent's home, while their youngest brother was still getting a tongue-lashing from their mother.

"We heard," said Peter Jr. "It's all over town."

"Well that's just great," said Lydia with her hands in the air.

Peter Jr. and Paul had always defended their little brother. Especially since 100% of the fights he was involved in, he didn't start, but he always finished. However, the look on their mother's face told them to keep their mouths shut.

"So what are we going to do?" asked Lydia.

"I think I have a solution," said Peter. "Until we can find another school for Lazarus that will take him in the fall, I believe he should get himself a job."

"I agree," said Grandpa Angus. "The lad can help me train some of these young pups at my gym."

"Not what I had in mind Angus," said Peter.

The family patriarch turned to his second-born son. "Paul is Rebecca's father hiring?"

Rebecca was Paul's wife and her father owned a pig farm on the outskirts of the city.

"The lad is no farmer Peter," said Grand Pa Angus.

"Haven't you caused enough problems Da?" said Lydia.

"You're lucky your poor mum isn't here to hear you talk to me that way," said Angus. "She would pup you good."

"If she knew what a bad example you set for our sons, she wouldn't," said Peter.

"Grandda is not a bad example for me," said Lazarus. "And I don't want to work on no pig farm."

"Oh you don't do you?" said Peter. "And since when did you have a choice in the matter?"

"Maybe next time you will follow the example of our Lord and

Savior Jesus Christ and turn the other cheek," added Lydia. "Instead of using your fists to solve your problems."

There was a knock on the front door.

"I will get it," said Leah.

"Who could be visiting us at this time of day?" asked Grandpa Angus.

Leah suddenly returned to the kitchen with a confused look on her face.

"What is it Lass?" asked her father.

"There is a man at the door dressed in weird clothing Da," answered Leah. "He say that he is my Uncle Amos."

"It can't be," shouted Lydia.

Grandpa Angus immediately leaped up from his chair, but then regretted it, forgetting that he was no spring chicken. Lazarus helped him up and they walked together, followed by Peter, Lydia, Leah, Peter Jr., and Paul to greet the visitor. It turned out that it was none other than Uncle Amos Mackinnon.

"Amos?" said Angus. "Is it really you?"

"Aye Da," answered the buckskin clad wearing man. "It's me."

The thirty-year-old hugged his father for the first time in twelve years. It almost felt like an eternity. When Angus released his only son, Lydia hugged her younger brother, tears falling down her cheeks. Her husband and sons patiently waited their turn, while Leah hid behind her grandfather.

"I thought we would never see you again," said Lydia.

"I have so much to tell Sis," said Amos. "It's good to see you again Peter."

Peter Buchanan shook his long-lost brother-in-law's hand and almost winced at his grip.

"You have gotten stronger over the years," he said.

"I will take that as a compliment." Amos stopped and looked at his three nephews and niece for a moment. "I see the three lads I once knew, n the men who stand before me."

"Welcome home Uncle Amos," said Peter Jr. and Paul simultaneously.

Amos shook both their hands and was impressed with their grips. Lazarus stood there in awe for a moment, as he looked at the buck-skin-clad figure, who he hasn't seen since he was four years old.

"Let me look at you Lazarus," said Amos. "Last time I saw you, I was still able to carry you over my shoulders."

"I remember Uncle Amos," said Lazarus. "Is this what the soldiers in the Army wear?"

Amos laughed. "Good God, no lad, I left the Army back in 06." Before he explained further, Amos turned to Leah. "And just who is this pretty lass that stands before me?"

"I'm Leah."

"You have your mother's eyes," said Amos. "You were two years old the last time I saw you."

"Grand Da said you went off to the Army," said Leah.

"Aye," answered Amos. "I did."

"But if you have been out of the Army for about four years son," said Angus. "Where have you been?"

"Trapping," answered Amos. "I have been living in the Rocky Mountains, making a living as a trapper."

"Rocky Mountains?" said Lazarus. "You mean west of the Missis-sippi, where Lewis and Clark went?"

"Aye nephew," answered Amos. "And boy do I have stories to tell you."

2

TAKE ME WITH YOU

BEFORE EVERYONE GOT SETTLED IN, Amos went to his pack horses and with the help of his nephews, retrieved gifts for his family that he brought from the West. He presented to Peter and Lydia, a bear skin rug, while to Lazarus he gave a tomahawk.

"A Crow warrior gave that to me," he said. "It is one of my most prized possessions and I would consider it an honor for you to have it."

"Thank you Uncle Amos," said Lazarus.

For Leah, he had a buckskin dress made for women, obviously. The little teenager was so excited, that she couldn't wait to go to her room and try it on. Amos gave Peter Jr. and Paul two beaver-skinned hats each and last, but not least, a bear claw necklace for his father. Angus Mackinnon examined the gift before putting it around his neck.

"Must have been some big beast that you have gotten these from son," he said.

"Grizzly bear," responded Amos. "On its hind legs, its head could reach the ceiling." Everyone gasped.

"How did you survive out there Amos?" asked Lydia.

Her brother just smiled. "Thank Christ for the right people in my life," he answered.

"Learned a lot from a fellow, named John Colter who rode with the Lewis & Clark Expedition and I had been living with the Crow."

"Crow?" asked Lazarus.

"A tribe of Indians who live around the Yellowstone region," said Amos. "Proud people, who make good friends, but they like to steal a lot though."

Lydia and Leah were a little confused by the last statement. Amos suddenly chuckled which caused a domino effect and everyone laughed as if he just told a joke.

Leah suddenly noticed a scar across his forehead and inquired about it.

"Difference of opinion with a Blackfoot warrior, my niece," said Amos. "He thought my scalp would look pretty hanging from his belt, but I thought otherwise."

Amos chuckled again, which caused everyone except Peter and Lydia to laugh.

"Then again, I took his scalp and hung it on my belt." Amos suddenly opened his buckskin jacket and exposed the scalp lock hanging from his belt.

"Wow," exclaimed Lazarus. "Can I touch it, Uncle?"

"Sure lad."

Lydia looked on in horror as she watched her son touch what had been the hair of another person. Granted she nor her husband had ever met an Indian, and all that they and their children knew about them was from what they read in the newspapers and neighbors who served in the Army and fought against them during the Revolutionary War. None of what they heard was positive.

"What is it like out there Uncle Amos?" asked Lazarus.

"The Garden of Eden lad," answered Amos. "The Highlands of Scotland itself can't even compare."

"Now I resent that," said Grand Pa Angus in mock anger.

Out of the entire family, he was the most quiet as he listened to his son explain about the West and could understand why he loved it.

He knew that Amos was not the same person that he was when he left for the army twelve years ago.

"Now that you're home Amos," said Peter. "What is it that you intend to do?"

Amos looked at his brother-in-law and smiled. "While I am proud and will always call you my family," he said. "This is no longer my home."

"What do you mean?" asked Lydia.

"I'm only here just to visit," answered Amos. "In about a week or so, I am heading back."

"You can't be serious," said Paul.

"Aye nephew, I am."

Lydia and Peter didn't know what to say. Amos was a grown man now, old enough to make his own decisions. Angus seemed to accept what his son had become and couldn't have been more proud, but he sensed that Amos had a much deeper reason to return to the frontier and it was more than just an adventure.

"What is her name son?" he asked.

Amos smirked and blushed. "Plain Feather," he finally said. "I have been courting her for almost a year."

Angus Mackinnon grinned, however, his daughter and son-in-law were another story.

"Plain Feather?" said Peter. "What kind of name is that for a white woman?"

"Never said she was white," responded Amos.

A shocked look suddenly appeared on Peter's face. "You're my sister's husband Peter," said Amos. "But if I were you, I would choose my next words carefully."

"Amos!!" shouted Lydia.

"I think your brother means it lass," said Angus.

"Now let everyone just calm down," said Peter Jr. "Da meant no offense Uncle Amos."

Amos looked between his nephews and his brother-in-law, before the latter quickly apologized.

"I truly meant no offense, Amos," said Peter. "Just surprised is all."

"Well it does get lonely out west," responded Amos in a calm tone.

"In speaking of women," said Leah. "Paul got married last summer."

"Did he now?" said Amos. "Congratulations, nephew."

"Thank you," said Paul.

"I hope you can meet her and her family before you leave."

"I don't see why not."

"Lazarus is going to be working for her Da on their pig farm," Leah blurted out.

"Thanks, sis," said Lazarus with a sigh.

"Did I come home at the wrong time?"

"Is there ever a right time?" asked Angus.

Peter and Lydia explained about their youngest son's expulsion from school and that working for Paul's father-in-law on his pig farm, until they can find him another school, would do him some good. Amos immediately felt for his youngest nephew, especially after he heard his side of the story.

"Lazarus is no farmer," said Amos.

"Funny," said Grandpa Angus. "That's what I said."

"Well Amos, when you have your own children, you can raise them and discipline them as you see fit," said Lydia.

"Lazarus needs to learn some discipline and respect for authority," added Peter.

"He also needs to stand up for himself," responded Amos. "Especially against bullies like this Marcus Rhodes fellow."

"Thank you, Uncle," said Lazarus.

"Look I'm not trying to tell you how to raise your children," said Amos. "But I have seen a lot in my travels, what the real world out there is like and it is not the kind of place, where you turn the other cheek and expect to survive."

"Maybe out west where you live among ruffians and savages

Amos," scoffed Peter. "But this is a civilized society and Lazarus needs to learn to respect it, if he is to ever succeed in it."

Amos looked at his brother-in-law and his sister for a minute.

"A society that thrives on human slavery is not what I would call civilized," he finally said.

"Uh-oh," said Peter Jr.

"We don't own any slaves Amos," said Lydia.

"Paul's in-laws do Mum," Leah said all of a sudden.

"Thank you Leah," said Lydia with sarcasm.

"In speaking of which," said Paul suddenly. "I better head home."

"Me too," said Peter Jr.

"See you lads tomorrow," said their father.

While Peter Buchanan Jr. was still single, he had saved up enough money to live in his own place in town, not far from his father's cordwainer shop. After dinner, Amos regaled tales of his adventures to the rest of his family well into the night, until it was just him, his father, and his nephew by the fireplace.

"The west must be some place son," said Angus. "I'm glad that you have found a place you can call home."

"Thank you Da," said Amos. "That means a lot to me."

Lazarus was quiet as he sat between his grandfather and uncle by the fireplace. The stories about the majestic Rockies and the people who lived there, as his uncle described it, played over and over again in his head. He imagined himself going west and becoming a trapper, like his Uncle Amos and that's when it hit him.

"When are you leaving to return west Uncle Amos?"

"In a week," answered Amos. "Maybe two, why?"

"Take me with you," Lazarus suddenly burst out.

At first both his uncle and grandfather started to chuckle, but then stopped suddenly, when they realized that the boy was serious.

"Your mum and Da will have me hung, drawn, and quartered," said Amos.

"Please Uncle Amos," pleaded Lazarus. "I want to be a trapper like you, I know I can learn."

Amos had no doubt that his nephew had grit, but that's not what concerned him.

"Lazarus," he said. "Have you ever killed a man?"

"Of course not."

"Be grateful that you have not," said Amos.

"Your Uncle is right lad," added Grandpa Angus. "I can't imagine what it was like when you took your first life son."

"It's not something that I am proud of Da," said Amos. "But it had to be done."

"Then why still live out there?" asked Lazarus.

Amos was quiet for a minute before he answered. "Freedom," he finally said. "True freedom."

Lazarus didn't bother asking his uncle what he meant by that, he automatically understood, based on what his uncle had told him about his life on the frontier.

"That is what I want uncle," he said. "I will never get it, as long as I live here."

Amos was about to deny his nephew, but then stopped and looked into his eyes. He then looked up into the eyes of his father, who was reading his thoughts.

"I wasn't that much older than him when I left home to find my own way in the world," Angus finally said.

Amos sucked his teeth. "If I take you with me, we may have to leave sooner than I had hoped."

"Why?" asked Lazarus.

"Do you really think your mum and dad are just going to let me take you west with me, without a fight?"

"Oh," was all Lazarus said.

His grandfather just chuckled. "You sure want to leave with your uncle, Lazarus?" he asked.

"Aye GrandDa," answered Lazarus.

"I will handle your sister and brother-in-law," said Angus. "You can announce it tomorrow evening when we eat at Paul and Rebecca's family's house."

"Thanks, Da," said Amos.

"Thank you, Uncle Amos," shouted Lazarus. "You won't regret it!"

"Keep it down lad," said Amos. "And I will hold you to that."

"It's getting late now," said Angus to Lazarus. "Time for you to go to bed."

Lazarus hugged his grandfather and uncle, before running up the stairs to his room. Once he was gone, Angus looked at his only son.

"Promise me that you will look out for him," he said. "For your sister's sake."

"With my life, Da," responded Amos. "I swear it on mum's grave."

3

THE JOURNEY BEGINS

LAZARUS ANNOUNCED his intentions of going with his uncle back west at Paul's in-laws home during dinner. To say that Lydia was angry would be the mother of all understatements. Paul had his father-in-law's servants remove the dinner utensils and any and everything not tied down that his mother could use as a potential weapon against her brother. Peter Buchanan was the opposite of happy also, but after calming his wife down, with the help of her father, it was clear to him that his youngest son had made his decision.

"I'm sorry Mum and Da," said Lazarus. "But I can't stay here, I am a man now and a man needs his freedom."

"But Lazarus," responded Lydia. "You don't know what you're getting yourself into or what you will run into out west."

"A man can't know what his life is meant to be if doesn't walk ahead with one foot in front of the other," responded Lazarus.

Lydia was almost in tears. Peter tried to comfort her as best as he could, before turning his attention towards his son and his brother-in-law.

"You sure about this son?"

Lazarus nodded.

"I will not only teach him," said Amos. "But I will look out for him, you have my word on that."

"I will hold you to it Amos," said Peter.

"Trust me Peter, you won't be the only one," said Amos.

"He swore on his mother's grave," added Angus. "He will lookout for Lazarus."

"Wait a minute," said Peter Jr. "You knew about this Grand Da?"

"Aye."

"When were you planning on telling us this?" asked Peter in even even-handed tone.

Angus Mackinnon just shrugged. "Oh, the day they were leaving I suppose."

Lydia's blood pressure went up as her husband tried to calm her down again, while both Peter Jr., Paul, and Paul's in-laws were chuckling. However, Lazarus's brothers came to his and their uncle's defense.

"Mum, Da," said Paul. "Lazarus is not a boy anymore, he is a man now."

"He is sixteen," retorted Lydia.

"That's how old you were when you married Da," said Peter Jr.

Both Angus and Peter Sr. smiled. "He got us there buttercup," said Peter Sr.

For the first time, Lydia was quiet. She looked at her youngest son and was starting to realize that he was not a baby anymore. Then she looked at her brother. She remembered when he was her son's age and she used to babysit him and look after him until he came of age.

"Promise me, Amos," she finally said. "You will watch out for him."

"On our Mum's grave," said Amos. "I will give my life to protect him."

"And I will do the same for you Uncle Amos," said Lazarus.

"I believe you," said Amos. "I pray you will never have to though."

At the end of the third week of January, Amos was packed and ready to return west. Lazarus, who didn't have much to begin with, was ready and eager as well. The family, with the exception of Lydia, was there to see them off.

"You sure about this son?" asked Peter.

Lazarus nodded. "Tell Mum I love her, always."

Peter nodded and hugged his son tight. Peter Jr. and Paul shook their hands and wished him and their Uncle Amos well. Leah and Rebecca, who were both in tears hugged both Lazarus and Amos, almost unable to let them go.

"Promise you will come visit," said Rebecca. "It will please both your brother and me that our baby will get a chance to meet their uncle and granduncle."

"Baby?" said Peter.

"Aye Da," said Paul. "You're going to be a Grand Da and you and Great Grand Da!" "

Congratulations!" shouted Amos. "God willing, we return for a visit to see my grandnephew or grand-niece."

Amos then turned to his father and hugged him. Lazarus followed suit.

"Stay alive out there," said Angus. "The both of you are all that you have now."

"We will Grand Da," said Lazarus. After hugging his grandfather, Lazarus mounted his horse, followed by his Uncle Amos. They said their final goodbyes to their kin and rode west.

"How long will it take us to reach St. Louis?" asked Lazarus.

"Depends," said Amos. "Barring any delays and as long as the weather remains agreeable, I would say maybe a month, or a month and a half."

"Will we at least reach the Rockies before summer?"

"That is the plan nephew," answered Amos.

Amos looked at the rifle that his nephew was carrying. It was an 1803 Harper's Ferry rifle that his grandfather bought him five years ago.

"Your grandfather got you that rifle?"

"Aye," answered Lazarus. "Paul and I used to go hunting a lot."

"Used to?"

"Since he got married and taken up farming, he hasn't had the time," said Lazarus. "So I would go with Grand Da during the summer or when we have free time."

"You will have plenty of free time to hunt Lazarus," said Amos.

"What are the animals like?" asked Lazarus. "Are they as big as you say they are?"

"Aye," answered Amos. "The buffalo is about three times the size of a horse and they are quite tasty."

Lazarus already pictured a herd of buffalo on the prairie in his mind and camping by a lake with his uncle, learning the trapping trade.

"Tell me more about the beaver," he asked.

"You mean how to trap them?"

"Aye."

"I will not lie to you nephew," said Amos. "It is back-breaking work, you're up to your knees in freezing water, searching for prime beaver hunting grounds. Plus you have to keep a lookout, before, during, and after you set your traps for deadly grizzly bears and hostile Indians." Amos paused for second and turned to see if he had his nephew's undivided attention. He was pleased to see that he did.

"It's as dangerous as you say it is?" asked Lazarus.

His uncle nodded. "Having second thoughts?"

Lazarus shook his head and smiled. "I have come this far," he said. "I might as well go all the way."

Lazarus paused for a moment. "Besides," he said. "You will need someone that you can trust to watch your back."

Amos beamed with pride at his nephew. "I appreciate that Lazarus," he said. "That means a lot."

"I have some questions about the Indians," said Lazarus.

"I will answer them the best way I know how," responded Amos. "What is it about them you wish to know?"

Lazarus paused for a moment and then with a sheepish grin, asked his question. "What are the women like?"

Amos suddenly guffawed.

4

MEETING A LEGEND

"If God will only forgive me this time and let me off, I will leave the country the day after tomorrow and be damned if I ever come into it again," John Colter at Three Forks, Montana, April of 1810.

Amos and Lazarus arrived in St. Louis by the end of April. During their travels, they hunted and camped, in order to save money from staying in Inns that were up and down the Ohio River and camping and sleeping under the stars in any kind of weather, helped prepare Lazarus for his life as a trapper in the Rockies. When they arrived in St. Louis, the first item of business on Amos's mind was to buy traps and other supplies for the journey.

Amos Mackinnon had been a free trapper since before he left the mountains to visit his kin back east and he had informed his nephew that the life of a free trapper was the life to live. Never be beholden to a company. Amos managed to save money from both his years in the Army and his life as a trapper, to help him continue to support himself and he planned on sharing that knowledge with his nephew and new apprentice.

"Where are we going to find a person to buy traps from Uncle Amos?" asked Lazarus.

"There are a lot of traders in St. Louis and retired trappers who are willing to sell traps," answered Amos. "Trick is, just knowing where to look."

The first person Amos had in mind to seek out was Manuel Lisa, one of the chief owners of the newly formed Missouri Fur Company. However, the Spaniard had already left St. Louis for Fort Lisa a couple of weeks previously and he wouldn't return until autumn. As the uncle and nephew were buying needed supplies other than traps for their journey, Amos saw someone, he thought he would never see again.

"John Colter!" he shouted. "Is it really you?"

The legendary mountain man and veteran of the Corps of Discovery turned around at the sound of his name. He smiled as he quickly recognized the Scotsman.

"As I live and breathe," he said. "Amos Mackinnon!"

The two friends shook hands and hugged each other as if they were long-lost brothers and had reunited at a family function. Amos quickly introduced his nephew. Now John Colter was no small man, but even he found himself looking up at the sixteen-year-old nephew of his friend and former trapping buddy. Lazarus offered his hand to Colter, who immediately shook it and was impressed with the teenager's grip.

"Now that's a firm handshake you have there young man," said Colter. "Tells me a lot about a man."

"Thank you, Mr. Colter," said Lazarus.

"Please," said Colter. "Call me John."

"So when did you get back in town?" asked Amos.

"Arrived this morning," answered John. "You?"

"Day before yesterday," said Amos.

"You heading back west?" asked John.

"Aye," answered Amos. "Taking me nephew with me, so he can learn to become a mountain man like us."

"I am not a mountain man, anymore Amos," said John Colter suddenly. "I'm done with the mountains."

Amos was a little surprised. About 90% of all the things he learned as a trapper, he learned from John Colter, not to mention John Colter was the toughest and bravest man that he knew.

"This wouldn't have anything to do with what happened between you and the Blackfeet last year would it?" asked Amos.

"Part of it," answered John. "Why don't we discuss this over lunch, it's on me."

John Colter took Amos and Lazarus to a small tavern by the docks. As they were waiting for their orders, John explained what happened almost a month ago.

"Last fall I was on my way back here to St. Louis when I ran into Manuel Lisa and his new partner Andrew Henry."

"I remember," said Amos. "We were at the Mandan village, knowing Lisa, he probably wanted you to take him and his men back to Fort Raymond."

"Nope," said Colter. "He wanted me to take them to Three Forks."

Amos's eyes nearly popped out of their sockets in shock. He remembered what happened to John and that idiot John Potts when they decided to go up to Three Forks to trap beaver. That was Black-foot country and Amos remembered George Droulliard warning both Colter and Potts that to voluntarily go into Blackfoot country to trap beaver was both foolish and suicidal.

"After what happened to you and Potts last year," said Amos. "I wouldn't have expected Manuel Lisa of all people to be that crazy."

"Neither did I," responded Colter. "But both he and Henry were determined to go, no matter the consequences, and since I was the only person who knew where Three Forks was, they begged me to take them."

"What is so special about this Three Forks?" asked Lazarus.

"If you ever want to find a place that is guaranteed to be chock full of beaver," said John Colter. "That is the place."

"The problem is that it is in the heart of Blackfoot country," said Amos.

"How come the Blackfoot don't want us trapping beaver?" asked Lazarus.

"They don't want us trapping beaver in their country, which I can understand," said Colter.

"I can understand that too," added Amos. "But I also heard from my Crow friends that the beaver is sacred to the Blackfoot."

"I heard that too," responded Colter. "You think after two damn near-death experiences with those sons of bitches, I would've learned." The trio chuckled for a minute.

"But they convinced you to guide them?" "Actually it was George who convinced me," said John.

"Droulliard?" said Amos. "Don't tell me he went with you to Three Forks."

Colter nodded. Amos shook his head. "What made you finally decide to quit the mountains?"

"The Blackfoot as usual," answered John. "We built a new fort at Three Forks, and spent the winter there, while Lisa went back to St. Louis for supplies."

When the server brought the men their lunch, they chowed down, except John Colter. He was still in thought for a while before he touched his food. Amos and Lazarus noticed this but were wise enough to keep quiet and continue eating. When John started to eat, he took his time. Amos could see that the events over the past year had a negative effect on his friend.

He had seen that before with war veterans, who have survived death one too many times. Amos was at Fort Raymond, when John Colter and John Potts left to go trapping at Three Forks. He remembered when John Colter showed up at the fort, a month later, buck naked and completely emaciated. Both he, Lisa, and Droulliard were there to bring him in and nurse him back to health.

John Colter rarely spoke about what happened to him and Potts the previous spring at Three Forks. Later that summer, he finally opened up to Amos about what the Blackfoot did. As he and Potts were traveling up the Jefferson River, they stumbled upon several hundred Blackfoot warriors who were not happy that the two trappers were in their territory. They signaled them ashore, in which Colter obeyed, but Potts was another story.

As the Blackfoot warriors took Colter ashore, Potts refused and tried to escape. According to Colter, one of the warriors shot and wounded Potts, who then returned fire and killed the warrior from the canoe. Before Potts had a chance to think, he was turned into a pin cushion by the Blackfoot, or as John Colter put it, "riddled with arrows."

Potts' body was then brought to shore, where it was cut to pieces. For John Colter, the Blackfoot had plans for him. When the leader of the war party asked the trapper through sign language, if he could run, Colter shook his head no. The truth was that Colter could run, but he was not about to tell a whole war party of bloodthirsty Blackfoot warriors that. With that in mind, they decided to make it a game and forced the trapper to run. What happened next would be the stuff of legend.

John Colter, completely naked, ran for his life. The Blackfoot gave him a headstart, and when they started to chase him, he knew this was not a game. He was completely naked and was running through cactus, briars, and other prickly plants native to the area, he started to bleed through his nose, but he continued to run, for he knew if he stopped, even for a moment, he was dead.

He outran all but one of his pursuers. A lone Blackfoot warrior was gaining on Colter, to the point, that the trapper could actually hear him breathing behind him. Completely exhausted, Colter stopped and faced the lone Blackfoot. The warrior in mid-run tried to stab Colter with his spear, but the trapper sidestepped him, causing the warrior to fall. Colter then grabbed the spear and killed the warrior.

Not wanting to check his handy work, John Colter continued to run, but this time, he needed to find a place to hide. He could no longer, outrun the Blackfoot, who were now really out for blood when they came upon their comrad's body. John Colter made it to the Madison River and swam to a beaver lodge, where he hid. The Blackfoot warriors searched the area to no avail. Colter hid in the beaver lodge until nightfall, then he emerged and traveled eleven days from the Madison River to Fort Raymond on the Little Big Horn.

Amos never forgot that story, especially after how John told him about it. It was the main reason, he never went trapping into Blackfoot country.

Fighting the Blackfoot was unavoidable since they were a war-like tribe, who raided other tribes, for horses, women, scalps, or all three. Some of those tribes, like the Crow and Flathead, Amos was good friends with and had fought by their side against the Blackfoot. But to willfully go into Blackfoot country to trap the beaver, which was considered sacred to that tribe, was foolish. It was one of the reasons Amos managed to survive out on the frontier and he planned on teaching Lazarus the same lesson.

"I take it there is no way I can talk you out of going back west is there?" asked John Colter.

"Not a chance John," answered Amos. "But I assure you, we will not be trapping in Blackfoot country, not if we can help it."

Lazarus nodded in agreement with his uncle.

"At least you're being smarter than I was," said John.

"I ain't never met a man smarter than you John Colter," said Amos. "You taught me just about everything I need to know about being a trapper."

"That may be," said Colter. "Don't mean I didn't make my share of mistakes and going back up to Three Forks last month was one of them."

"Everyone makes mistakes," said Lazarus. "The key is to learn from them and others."

Both John Colter and Amos looked at Lazarus. "How old are you Lazarus?" asked John.

"Sixteen."

"You sure don't act like it."

"Thanks, I guess." Amos just chuckled as he beamed at his nephew.

"The lad has all the makings of a mountain man."

"I think your right Amos," added John.

It was quiet again for a moment. "When you boys headed out?" asked John.

"Soon as we can find someone to sell us some traps," added Amos. "I'll be damned if I work for a company."

"Well hell if it's traps that you need, why didn't you say so?" said John. "I got traps that I can sell you since I no longer have any need for them."

"Thank you," said Lazarus.

After they finished their lunch and Colter paid it, he took them to his canoe, which was laden with traps and beaver, from his last season. Amos still had plenty of money left and John Colter gave him and Lazarus a good price for the traps.

"Really appreciate this John," said Amos.

"Thank you for taking the traps off of my hands," said John.

The retired trapper turned to Lazarus to offer some very helpful advice. "Listen to your Uncle," he said. "His kind of wisdom will save your life."

"Thank you, John," said Lazarus. "I don't think I have a better teacher than him."

John Colter paused for a moment, then took out something from his belt. It was an Arkansas toothpick. "I want you to have this Lazarus," he said.

Lazarus just stood there in surprise, about to refuse the gift. "I haven't done anything to deserve this gift," he said.

"Other than your Uncle, I don't see anyone else more deserving of it," said John.

Lazarus looked at his uncle, who encouraged him to take it. The youth accepted the gift. He took the knife out of its sheath and examined it. The blade was slightly curved, but the lad could tell that it was sharp.

"Learn to use it, lad," said John. "Out on the frontier, things can get very personal."

"I will John and thank you," said Lazarus. "I will never forget this."

John Colter said his goodbye to Amos Mackinnon and Lazarus Buchanan and wished them well, before going into the city to find his friend and former Corps of Discovery commander William Clark. Having everything they needed for the journey, Amos and Lazarus decided to leave the next morning. Their adventure was about to begin.

5

WHERE THE BUFFALO ROAM

THE DUO LEFT ST. Louis the very next day. Amos took the lead, while Lazarus pulled the two-pack mules that his uncle bought, which were laden with supplies and traps. They followed the Missouri River from St. Louis, traveling at least twenty miles a day. Sometimes they would feast on beans, biscuits, and salt pork when they camped, but most of the time, when they weren't traveling they managed to hunt and snag a deer, an antelope, or two.

While growing up in Delaware, Lazarus, used to hunt with his brothers and grandfather, so he knew how to skin and dress game. He was looking forward to seeing his first buffalo, but Amos advised patience. The Missouri River was the longest river in the United States, flowing east to south at 2,341 miles before entering the Gulf of Mexico. To get to their destination, which was Crow country near the Yellowstone region, it would take the duo at least a month and a half to go by land on horseback.

Lazarus tried his best to not let the daily monotony of riding the endless prairie while following the river get to him. He did not slacken in his duties and at his uncle's insistence, cleaned and checked his weapons thoroughly and was always aware of his surroundings. It wasn't until the third week of the month of May, when they were near what is now Sioux City, Iowa, that they finally saw their first herd of buffalo.

Amos called a halt as he and his nephew stared at what looked to be close to a thousand, maybe more individuals buffalo bulls, cows, and calves, grazing on the endless prairie. Some were going down to the river to drink. Lazarus just stood on his horse and looked in sheer, dumb-struck awe.

"You were right Uncle," he said. "They are three times the size of a horse."

"Told ya, didn't I?" chuckled Amos. "We'll move further up from the herd, so they don't smell us."

"Aren't we going to hunt one?"

"Of course we are lad," answered Amos. "But first things first."

Lazarus knew better than to question his uncle's judgment, so he followed his lead to where they were going to set up camp.

"We only have one pack animal enough to carry meat from one of those tasty animals," said Amos. "So we will only shoot one animal, preferably a cow."

"We'll we need more horses Uncle?" asked Lazarus.

"Aye," answered Amos. "But we should be able to trade for some horses with a friendly tribe before we reach the Crow nation."

Among the three horses that Amos had bought in St. Louis, two of them were laden with rifles and gunpowder. He knew that those were a valuable commodity on the frontier for the tribes. He planned on trading for more horses with those weapons, with the Crow or Flathead, once he and Lazarus arrived at their destination, but the Omaha, Iowa, Osage, and Pawnee tribes who often frequented this area would do as well. Once they got the camp set up, Amos had Lazarus bring the two pack mules and a pack horse and follow him.

"You're going to hunt your first buffalo nephew," he said. "Now I need you to pay close attention because on occasions like this, it could be a matter of life or death, especially during starving times."

"Lead the way Uncle," said Lazarus.

They were downwind from the herd. Amos reminded his nephew that they were going to shoot only one animal since they had enough pack animals to carry meat from just one adult buffalo. Since Lazarus had never hunted buffalo before, Amos would do the honors this time. He informed his excited nephew that he would get his chance.

Amos picked out a lone adult cow from the herd, checked his prime from his Kentucky long rifle, put a bead on his target, breathed in, and fired. The musket ball found its mark. The buffalo cow went down convulsing.

"Let's go lad," said Amos.

Lazarus followed his uncle to the downed cow. He was amazed that the herd was not disturbed by them or that one of their comrades was shot down. Amos immediately started gutting the cow, pulling out her, heart, liver, intestines, kidneys, and cut out her tongue, putting the steaming organs on a canvas that he and Lazarus laid out on the ground to keep them from getting dirty and contaminated. Before he went to skinning the animal, Amos with a wicked grin, picked up the buffalo heart and took a bite. Lazarus just stood there in shock at his uncle. After he took another bite, Amos offered the steaming organ to his nephew.

"But it is not even cooked," said Lazarus.

"Doesn't matter lad," answered Amos. "Taste better when it is raw, plus the tribes do this after a hunt."

"They do?"

"Aye lad," answered Amos. "If you want to learn how to survive out here, do what the Indians do."

Lazarus thought for a moment, then decided to accept the buffalo heart. He took a bite.

"Well lad," said Amos. "What do you think?"

Lazarus had to stop himself from retching at first while chewing on the piece of raw meat. Once he swallowed, he took another bite, chewed, and then smiled.

"Tastes better than chicken!"

Amos laughed and patted his nephew on the back. They finished the buffalo heart together, before skinning the rest of the cow, which took time, even with the pack animals pulling the skin off. By the time they were done, they had all the choicest meats cut up in the canvas tarp and covered in the buffalo robe. They left the rest of the carcass to the scavengers and returned to their camp. Lazarus volunteered to cook, but his uncle refused and volunteered.

"I believe it is my turn to cook lad," said Uncle Amos. "Besides you don't know how to cook boudins."

"What are those?"

"Buffalo sausage," answered Uncle Amos. "My favorite meat from the buffalo, you're in for a treat lad."

Boudins were a kind of sausage that was a delicacy among French trappers. The French fur trapper Toussaint Charbonneau prepared boudin blanc for Lewis and Clark on their expedition. It is made up of buffalo intestine, meat, kidney, and suet, boiled as links, then fried in bear grease. While Amos didn't have any bear grease, he did have grease from the settlements and used that to fry the boudins.

Once they were cooked, he gave Lazarus one to try. The youth took a bite, chewed for a while, savoring the tender meat, and swallowed. He responded with a smile.

"Ye missed your calling Uncle," he said. "You should have been a cook."

"I will take that as a compliment, nephew," said Amos. "More?"

"Aye, but not too much," said Lazarus. "I mean you still need to eat too."

Both uncle and nephew laughed as the former served two more boudin blanc to his nephew. After dinner, Lazarus took the plates and utensils to the river to wash them. Amos warned him to be careful and check his pistols. Ever the apt student, Lazarus took his uncle's advice to heart and checked his pistols, making sure that they were loaded and primed, just in case, before taking the plates and utensils to the river.

Once he got to the river, Lazarus looked around and made sure that he was not being watched, or that he didn't have any unwanted visitors. He remembered his uncle telling him that grizzly bears, especially mothers with cubs, frequented the rivers near bushes. The youth had yet to see his first grizzly bear and based on what his uncle told him about them, he wasn't that eager to encounter one.

He quickly knelt down and washed the plates and utensils with the lye soap he bought in St. Louis. When his chore was completed, he stood up and was shocked to find that he was not alone. Across the river staring right back at him were two Indians. One, a man, armed with a lance and the other a woman. Neither one appeared to be in a threatening manner, so Lazarus outwardly remained calm.

Inwardly was another matter. After about a minute, Lazarus calmly waved at the couple and then with the plates and utensils in hand, slowly turned around and walked back to camp. He stopped only once to look over his shoulder to see if the Indian couple were still there. They weren't. When he got back to camp, he informed his uncle what he saw.

6

FIRST BLOOD

EARLY THE NEXT MORNING, as they were breaking camp, Lazarus and his uncle had visitors. A group of warriors rode in. Lazarus immediately recognized one of the men as the warrior he had seen last night and told his uncle as much. Amos nodded, before offering the peace sign. The leader of the warriors responded in kind.

"Who are they Uncle?" asked Lazarus.

"Omaha."

"Are they friendly?"

"Aye," answered Amos. Amos never took his eye of off the leader as he continued to speak to him in sign.

"I am Yellow Bull," signed the leader. "Why are you in the land of my people?"

"We are traveling through," answered Amos. "Going to the land of the Apsaalooke."

Yellow Bull nodded.

Amos could tell that Yellow Bull and his warriors were not a war party, but a hunting party. The warrior that Lazarus saw the night before walked up next to Yellow Bull, said something to him, and pointed at the teenager.

"What is he saying?" asked Lazarus.

"I don't speak Omaha lad," answered Amos. "Just be patient and don't do anything stupid."

"Is this man a relative of yours?" asked Yellow Bull in sign.

Amos smiled and nodded. "He is the son of my sister," he answered. "I am taking him to the land of the Apsaalooke to learn to become a trapper."

"My brother and his woman saw him last night," said Yellow Bull.

"I know," responded Amos. "He told me."

"How are you called?"

"There are no words in your tongue for my name," said Amos.

Then he said his name in English. Yellow Bull tried to pronounce it but had great difficulty.

"We white men have very strange names," said Amos.

For the first time, Yellow Bull and his warriors laughed and smiled.

"I'm sure that our names are strange to you white men," said Yellow Bull's brother in sign. Amos chuckled in agreement.

"I am called Raven," said Yellow Bull's brother. Amos offered his hand to Raven, who appeared to be younger than Yellow Bull.

"It's a pleasure to meet you," said Amos. "Lazarus introduce yourself."

"How?"

"Don't worry lad," assured Amos. "I will translate in sign."

Lazarus introduced himself to Raven and his brother Yellow Bull and apologized to the former if he was rude to him and his woman the night before. Raven smiled and accepted the youth's apology.

"This is your first time in our lands?" asked Raven.

Lazarus nodded. "My uncle is going to teach me how to trap beaver."

Amos translated his nephew's statement. Both Yellow Bull and Raven looked approvingly at the youth. They could tell that Amos Mackinnon was a seasoned trapper and had dealt with Indians before. They could also tell that the Scotsman while, not a man you should mess with, but also a man of honor. Amos was getting the same feeling about them when suddenly one of the warriors shouted something in the Omaha language and pointed north.

Coming over the horizon, was another band of Indians and they were painted for war.

"Sioux!!" shouted Yellow Bull.

"Lazarus get your guns and follow me," shouted Amos.

Lazarus did not question his uncle. He did immediately as he was told and got his weapons. Yellow Bull immediately was shouting orders at his warriors and they got into a defensive position, to prepare for the oncoming war party that was headed straight for them. Amos and Lazarus joined the Omaha warriors and signed to them that they would fight by their side.

The Sioux, whose real names were the Lakota, had been long-time enemies of the Omaha, and fighting between the tribes was always personal.

"It looks like we have a fight coming uncle," said Lazarus as he aimed his rifle at the oncoming party.

"Aye lad," said Amos. "Make your shots count."

"Who are they?"

"Lakota," answered Amos. "But their enemies call them the Sioux."

Lazarus just nodded. While the youth was afraid, he knew something like this was bound to happen sooner or later. He hoped that this would not be his last day on earth. As the Lakota war party got closer, Yellow Bull and his warriors, unleashed their arrows into them, while Amos and Lazarus fired.

Their action had the intended effect. A couple of the Lakota warriors were shot off their horses, before stopping and dismounting quickly to find cover. Some of the Lakota warriors had guns and returned fire, while the rest fired from their bows and arrows. In a split second, Lazarus noticed that one of the arrows was about to land where Yellow Bull was, and he immediately grabbed the Omaha leader and pulled him out of harm's way.

The Lakota arrow landed at the exact same spot, that Yellow Bull had just occupied. Before the Omaha leader had a chance to thank

Lazarus, their enemies charged. Amos managed to shoot the leader of the Lakota war party, before taking out his Crow tomahawk and an Arkansas toothpick, as he followed Raven and the Omaha war party to meet the enemy in hand-to-hand combat.

Yellow Bull quickly got up to his feet and helped Lazarus, before both of them followed the rest of the Omaha warriors into battle. The fighting was fast and fierce. Amos was fighting like a beserker, killing two enemy warriors in his wake, before another Lakota warrior managed to slash his side with a knife. The wound wasn't deep, but the Scotsman was enraged and was ready to face the Lakota warrior responsible. Before the warrior could even fight Amos though, a gunshot rang out and a brand new hole formed in the middle of the Lakota warrior's head. Amos turned around to see where the shot came from and he saw his nephew holding his smoking Harper's Ferry rifle in his hand.

"Now that is some lad," shouted a smiling Amos. Lazarus just stood there in shock for a moment, before coming back to his senses and saw two more enemy warriors coming straight for his uncle. "Uncle Amos," he shouted. "Behind you!!"

Amos quickly turned to face the two oncoming enemy warriors. However, he was joined by Yellow Bull, Raven, and three other Omaha warriors, followed by Lazarus, who had two of his pistols out. Without hesitation, he immediately cocked the hammer on both of his guns, aimed and fired at the two enemy combatants. The Lakota warriors were struck down where they stood.

Again Lazarus was in a little state of shock at what he just did, but was quickly brought back to his senses when Yellow Bull quickly patted him on the back. Lazarus looked at the Omaha warrior, who smiled at him and nodded his approval. The battle between Omaha and the Lakota shifted in the former's favor when one of the warriors was able to escape and get back to their village to retrieve more warriors.

As the fighting commenced, that warrior returned in no time with over a hundred Omaha warriors coming to the rescue. The Lakota seeing this, immediately retreated from the battlefield and hightailed it out of there. Yellow Bull shouted to the oncoming Omaha rescue party to follow the enemy and make sure that they didn't return. When the battle was over, there were at least twenty dead Lakota warriors and six Omaha. Despite the fierceness of the battle, Yellow Bull considered it good medicine, that he and his warriors didn't lose more men, and that his people won the day.

"This looks bad," said Lazarus as he checked his uncle's wound."

"It's just a scratch lad," said Amos.

As Lazarus washed his uncle's wound, he began to stitch it together. The youth had never done anything like this, so his uncle had to instruct him. Paying strict attention and carefully following his uncle's instructions, Lazarus managed to sow the wound closed, without difficulty. Yellow Bull and Raven approached to check on the duo.

"How did I do?" asked Lazarus.

Amos checked on his nephew's handiwork and smiled. "You did well lad," he said.

Yellow Bull also checked the wound and nodded his approval, before saying something in sign.

"He says that you are a true warrior," said Amos as he was translated. "You not only saved his life, but you fought like the white bear, killing your enemies without fear."

Lazarus did not know what to say. He wasn't sure if he deserved such praise. To make matters worse, his hands were shaking. Yellow Bull said something to him in sign.

"He asks if it is the first time you have killed a man," said Amos.

Lazarus nodded. "They were going to kill my uncle and they were your enemies," he said. He quickly stopped, as his hands continued to shake. Yellow Bull immediately grabbed the youth's hands to stop them from shaking. He looked into the youth's eyes and saw something. He smiled, before releasing Lazarus's hands.

"It will pass," he said in sign. Amos translated. "You fought in defense of a people you barely knew and risked your life for us, against our enemy."

Raven then approached and gave an eagle feather to the youth. Lazarus looked at his uncle.

"It is a sign of friendship lad," he said. "And it means that you are a warrior now."

Yellow Bull spoke in his language and used signs to translate.

"He says that he is in your debt for saving his life and for fighting for his people against an enemy," translated Amos.

Yellow Bull signed some more and Amos almost chuckled, but then stopped and beamed with pride at his nephew.

"He has given you a name."

"What is it?"

"White Bear," answered Amos. "He has called you White Bear."

Lazarus didn't know what to say, but at least his hands had stopped shaking.

"Thank you, Yellow Bull," he finally said. "I will always call the Omaha my friend." Amos translated in sign. This caused Yellow Bull and his warriors to whoop and cheer.

While Lazarus was glad that he was able to save his uncle's life and fight with their new friends against a common enemy, he was still troubled inside. He had drawn first blood, even though it was in battle and it was to save the life of another, it still bothered him. Amos, who was now standing, gently placed his hand on his nephew's shoulder.

"Don't let it get to you lad," he said. "It will pass."

"How did you get over your first kill?"

"By moving on," said Amos. "You have to if you're going to survive on the frontier."

"What if I can't?" asked Lazarus.

"You can lad," said Amos. "Yellow Bull told me so."

"How does he know?"

"Because he saw it in your eyes," answered Amos. "As did I, when you asked me to bring you out here to become a mountain man."

"You did?" asked a surprised Lazarus.

"Aye lad," answered Amos. "What you just did, took gumption and you have a lot of that."

Lazarus thought for a moment. He did what he had to do and plus since he begged his uncle to bring him and teach him the ways of a mountain man, he started to see things more clearly.

"The trick is lad is this," said Amos. "Don't take to like killing."

"I don't believe I could ever take to like killing another person," responded Lazarus.

"That is good to know lad," said Amos. " I have seen men who have gone from killing out of necessity to killing out of pure pleasure."

"I pray I never become such a man."

Amos smiled at his nephew and padded him on the back. "You and me both," he said.

At that point, Yellow Bull invited them to his village. Amos accepted.

"Shouldn't we be heading for Crow country?" asked Lazarus.

"No need to be in such a rush lad," answered Amos. "Besides we can open a trade with Yellow Bull's people and get some new horses out of it."

"Whatever you think it is best Uncle Amos," said Lazarus. The duo went back to their camp to retrieve their horses and belongings.

7

THE LESSONS BEGIN

AMOS AND LAZARUS spent a couple of days among the Yellow Bull's people. Amos managed to trade a crate of rifles and ammo for four horses. Also started learning sign language from his uncle and was able to test his knowledge of it with Raven and his wife Red Bird. Lazarus was trying to tell Raven that he is a lucky man to have a beautiful wife, but he mistranslated and accidentally said that he was lucky to have an old wife. Both the warrior and his wife chuckled, mainly because they knew the youth meant no insult and that he just started to learn sign language. When Uncle Amos corrected his nephew's error, the youth's embarrassment showed. However both Raven and his wife assured the youth that no offense was taken and that they knew he was still learning.

"In order for a man to grow, he must learn from his mistakes," said Raven in sign.

Amos translated the warrior's statement to Lazarus, which made the youth feel much better. Red Bird then said something to her husband, who just nodded in response. Amos asked in sign what Red Bird said and Raven told him, causing the Scotsman to chuckle.

"What is so funny?" asked Lazarus

"His wife says you need a good woman," answered Amos. "That way your sign language skills can get better, among other things."

Lazarus turned beet red, which caused his uncle and Raven to laugh.

As Lazarus' lessons were just beginning, one of the first things he learned about Indians, was that they have a huge sense of humor. At least that is what he was seeing from Yellow Bull's village. Everything that he ever heard about Indians while growing up back east, was mostly negative propaganda, however, he was grateful to see that at least among the Omaha, all the negative stories he had heard about Indians were mostly pure myth.

True they were different from whites and they often fought, but his kind was no different. Indians lived and fought to protect their loved ones, no differently than their white counterparts. As Lazarus was soon learning, especially from his Uncle Amos, walk a mile in another man's shoes, you will find that you have a lot more in common than you realized.

A couple of days later, just as Amos and Lazarus were about to continue on their journey, Yellow Bull, who as it turns out was a war chief in this Omaha village, gave Lazarus five horses as a token of appreciation for saving his life. The youth was dumbstruck, but he quickly learned that to refuse such a generous gift, would be an insult, so he accepted the horses and added them to the four horses that his uncle bought in trade for the crate of rifles and gunpowder. They said their goodbyes to the Omaha village of Yellow Bull, before riding out, heading north. While they were riding, Lazarus thought about his new name White Bear.

"Uncle Amos?"

"Aye," answered Amos.

"Why did Yellow Bull name me White Bear?" asked Lazarus. "Was it because of the way I fought against the Lakota?"

"It was part of it."

"What is the other part?"

Amos chuckled before answering. "Because of your white hair

and your pasty white skin," he said. "Not to mention, you're almost as big as the grizzly bear on its hind legs."

"But you have white hair and you're just as pasty white as me."

"Aye," said Amos. "But I already have an Indian name."

"You do?"

"Aye nephew," said Amos. "The Crow gave it to me a couple of summers ago."

"What is it?"

"White Horse Talker."

"Why did they give you that name?" asked Lazarus with a weird look.

"Well, other than my white hair and pasty white skin," said Amos. "I have a way with horses."

"Oh," was all Lazarus said.

The duo continued to travel north, following the Missouri River, bypassing the Mandan villages. When they saw more buffalo, this time a lot more than they saw, when they met the Omaha, they stopped to hunt. This time Lazarus was allowed to shoot first, remembering how his uncle did it. He took down a cow, then reloaded and repeated the process, this time taking down a bull.

Amos patted his nephew on the back, congratulating him. They spent most of the day butchering the two buffalos. By this time Lazarus had gotten used to eating buffalo heart and liver raw, much to his uncle's pride. What he was also getting better at, were the sign language lessons. During dinner, Amos would teach his nephew what certain tribes were in sign, as well as animals. Lazarus was also learning how to read signs. When things were quiet, that meant someone or something was in the area, that was not supposed to be there, or if something didn't smell right. If things were not quiet, usually, the birds were chirping and chipmunks and squirrels were running to and fro, making noises, which meant that all was well.

By the time they reached the Yellowstone River region, near the Little Bighorn, they were in Crow country and it was the first week of July. Lazarus was getting proficient in his sign language skills and he was getting better at reading signs, so his uncle decided to test him.

They came across a pile of what looked to be manure or scat. Amos had Lazarus check it out to see how fresh it was or how old. The youth reluctantly dismounted and put his finger in the scat to see how fresh it was.

"Well?" asked Uncle Amos.

"It seems to be cold," said Lazarus. "Maybe a couple of days."

"That looks just about right," beamed Amos. "Can I go wash my hands?"

Amos chuckled and nodded. The Scotsman recognized the scat to be from a bear. He could tell because of the amount of undigested fish eggs that were in it. Whether they were from a grizzly or a black bear, he couldn't tell. Either way, he was proud that his nephew was learning his lessons well, but he still had a long way to go. As the youth was returning from washing his hands, he suddenly stopped. Looking at the expression on his nephew's face, Amos turned around and quickly noticed that they weren't alone.

Just over the hill, they were being watched by a group of Indian warriors. Lazarus already knew that they were not a war party due to the fact that their faces weren't painted, but he also knew that didn't mean they were friendly. Either way, he would defer to his uncle.

"Who are they?" he asked as he rode up to his uncle.

"Crow." Lazarus relaxed a little.

"Didn't you tell me that you were courting a young lass from that tribe?"

"Aye nephew," answered Amos. "But whether these gentlemen are from her village or not, I can't tell from this distance, just keep your weapons at the ready."

"Why?"

"Because the Crow are expert horse thieves," answered Amos. "They love to steal horses, even from friends."

"That doesn't seem right," said Lazarus.

"To a white man's way of thinking it ain't," responded Uncle Amos. "But to their way of thinking, they see it as capturing."

"How do they see it as capturing another man's horse, even if that man is a friend?" asked a surprised Lazarus.

"Simple," said Amos. "If you can't take better care of looking out for your horse and you let it get stolen right out from under your nose, then it is your fault."

"Now that is a completely daft way of thinking," said Lazarus.

"Maybe," said Amos. "But it is their way of thinking, no matter how daft we think it is."

"And you're friends with them," said Lazarus.

"Aye," answered Amos. "At least they are honest about who they are and what they do with no shame, which is more than what I could say about our kind."

Lazarus pondered on that for a minute and was about to respond, but quickly kept his mouth shut as the crow warriors approached him and his uncle. He counted at least eight of them, so he could tell that this was not a war party, from his limited experience with Indians. He turned to his uncle and was surprised to see a smile on his face. He turned back to the crow warriors and saw that the leader was smiling back at his uncle.

"It is good to see you again White Horse Talker," said the leader in English.

"It is great to be back, Running Dog," said Amos. "It has been a long time."

8

THE CROW

THE CROW PEOPLE or Apsaalooke as they called themselves, had been living in the Yellowstone River region in what is now southern Montana since the late 18th century. Their territories were from what is now Yellowstone National Park in the west to the Musselshell River in the north, to the northeast at the mouth of the Yellowstone at the Missouri River, to all the way down to the Wind River Mountain Range in what is now the states of Montana and Wyoming.

Amos started trading with the Crow when he rode with John Colter and two other trappers in 1806. He has known Running Dog for about three years now. When Colter was on his way down to St. Louis and met Manuel Lisa, Amos stayed with the Crow and learned their culture and way of life, as well as their language. Before he left the mountains to return east and visit his kin, he was courting Running Dog's cousin Plain Feather. She would be eighteen summers now.

"How are your people Running Dog?" asked Amos in Crow.

"We have been well," answered Running Dog. "Winter was hard as usual, but the Creator has been good to us."

"And Plain Feather?"

Running Dog grinned. "She waits for you."

The Scotsman nodded and smiled. "I hope to speak with her father, Medicine Hawk, over an important issue."

Running Dog and the rest of the Crow hunting party laughed. They all guessed what Amos Mackinnon had in mind.

They turned their attention to Lazarus and Amos quickly introduced his nephew. "My brothers," he said in Crow. "This is the son of my sister, Lazarus."

Amos signaled Lazarus forward and the youth signed friend to the hunting party.

"Laaazaarrus," said Lame Deer. He was Running Dog's younger brother and knew some English, thanks to Amos. He appeared to be a couple of years older than Lazarus.

"You white men have strange names," he said in heavily accented English.

Both Amos and Lazarus chuckled. "So I have been told," responded Lazarus. "I have been given an Indian name."

Lame Deer and Amos translated the youth's last statement for those who didn't speak English. Running Dog spoke and understood the white man's tongue, but only spoke around white men that he trusted, like Amos.

"What name have you been given?" he asked in English.

"White Bear," answered Lazarus. "An Omaha war chief named Yellow Bull gave me that name after I had saved his life in battle with the Lakota."

Lazarus was using a sign as he spoke and his statement brought gasps and surprises from most of the Crow hunting party.

"My nephew speaks with a straight tongue," said Amos in Crow. "I also have the scar to prove it."

Both uncle and nephew explained about meeting the Omaha and their battle with the Lakota. It just so happens that the Crow were also enemies to the Lakota and when they heard how Lazarus killed three Lakota warriors in his first battle. Running Dog and Lame Deer were both impressed.

"Come," said Running Dog. "Our village is not far from here."

"Lead the way my brother," said Amos. "It will be nice to be among family and friends again."

They followed the hunting party about two miles from the Bighorn River, near what is now the Montana/Wyoming border. Like most tribes of the plains and Rocky Mountains, the Crow did not have a single chief who ruled over the entire tribe, but many villages had a leader who was a chief and even he didn't have total authority over the village.

The decisions were made by the counsel, in which the chief could suggest or give advice and it was up to the council to make the decisions. However if the chief was a proven and wise leader, then he was who the people followed. The main leader or head chief of this village was Medicine Hawk. He was in his early forties and a tall man at 5 feet, 11 inches, and weighed a muscular one hundred and seventy pounds.

While polygamy was practiced among the Crow tribe as with many tribes, Medicine Hawk was satisfied with only one wife, Blue Willow, and she was the mother of their five children. Three boys and two girls. Their eldest daughter was none other than Plain Feather, whom Amos Mackinnon had been courting for a year. The hunting party rode in, followed by Amos and Lazarus, and stopped in front of Chief Medicine Hawk's tipi to pay their respects to the Chief.

"It is good to have you back White Horse Talker," said Chief Medicine Hawk. "Who is your friend?"

"Chief Medicine Hawk," said Amos. "This is my nephew Lazarus."

Medicine Hawk looked approvingly at the youth. He was actually sizing him up as he usually does when he meets strangers or mostly white men.

"Lazarus, this is Medicine Hawk," said Amos. "He is the chief of this village."

"It is good to meet you and your people," said Lazarus in sign.

Medicine Hawk smiled. "Your use of sign is good," he said in a heavy accented English. Lazarus was surprised.

"You speak my tongue."

"I speak some," said Medicine Hawk. "Your Uncle is a good teacher."

"I agree," said Lazarus. "He is the best."

"My nephew has become a warrior," said Amos. "In the land of the Omaha, he killed three Lakota warriors in battle and saved the life of the Omaha chief Yellow Bull."

"This is good," said Medicine Hawk. "We should hold a feast and he should tell us this is."

Lazarus was a little embarrassed. Amos patted his nephew on the shoulder and encouraged him to show the Crow Chief the eagle feather that Raven gave him. Lazarus had already tied it to his wide-brim hat, before he and his uncle left the Omaha village. Medicine Hawk and the council, who by this time had come out and surrounded the newcomers, were impressed. It was at that moment, that Amos saw a sight that put a huge smile on his face.

"Plain Feather!!" he shouted.

The young daughter of Medicine Hawk and Blue Willow ran from behind her mother and hugged the Scotsman.

"I have prayed for your return White Horse Talker," said Plain Feather.

"I'm glad to be back." Amos then introduced Plain Feather to Lazarus. The youth bowed before her and she giggled.

"You have hair the same color as your uncle," she said in English. "Does your mother and father have hair white as snow?"

Lazarus, who had always been shy around women, just shook his head.

Amos just chuckled. "Only my father, myself, and my sister's son, have white hair." Amos then turned to Medicine Hawk and Blue Willow. "There is something I must discuss with you."

Medicine Hawk nodded and smirked. He guessed what Amos wanted to talk about. "We will discuss this later tonight."

Medicine Hawk had some of the village boys take Amos and Lazarus's

animals and belongings to a lodge that was being set up for them, while he invited the uncle and nephew to smoke the pipe with him.

Blue Willow brought her husband his pipe and filled it with kinnikin-nick. Medicine Hawk lit the pipe and pointed it to the four directions of earth and gave thanks to the creator for Amos's return and welcoming his nephew to the people.

He then smoked the pipe and then passed it to Amos. Lazarus watched his uncle repeat the process, before smoking it. This was the youth's second pipe ceremony, the first, being when he was with the Omaha and found it interesting that the Crow is no different. Amos passed the pipe to Lazarus, who repeated what he saw and thanked God for the safe journey and for making new friends.

Then he smoked and nearly coughed up a lung, eliciting laughter from his uncle and the chief, as well as those on the council. Lazarus smoked it some more and got the hang of it, before passing the pipe to Running Dog.

After the pipe ceremony questions were asked about the past winter and spring and how Amos's journey to visit his kin in the east went. Then Amos explained how his nephew begged him to bring him out west and train him to be a trapper and then talked about John Colter leaving the mountains, after leading a trapping expedition into Three Forks.

"Why do you white men go into the Blackfoot country to trap the flattail, knowing how dangerous it is?" asked Running Dog.

"Simple," answered Amos. "Because we are either stupid, greedy or both!"

Everyone laughed. Amos also spoke in a sign for Lazarus's benefit.

"We have heard that white men are going into Three Forks," said Medicine Hawk. "Most never return."

"Not surprised," said Amos. "When we saw Colter in the land of the whites, he told us that Drouillard went into Three Forks with the trapping expedition."

All of a sudden it was quiet. Most of the Crow warriors knew George Drouillard, just as much as they knew John Colter and Amos Mackinnon.

"You don't know?" said Medicine Hawk.

"Know what?"

"A couple of moons ago," said Medicine Hawk. "Some white men, who were heading east, visited us from the fort that was built in Three Forks."

"What did they say?" asked Amos.

Medicine Hawk was quiet for a minute but decided to come out and say it. "They said Drouillard is dead," he finally said. "They found his body not far from the fort, the Blackfoot had taken his head, while his stomach was cut open and his insides were left for the vultures and wolves."

Amos just lowered his head and shook it. Other than John Colter, George Drouillard was also a good friend of his.

"Damn him!!" he shouted. "What was that fool doing in Three Forks anyway?"

"I'm sorry Uncle Amos," said Lazarus.

"It can't be helped Lazarus," said Amos. "Let this be a lesson to you."

"Trapping beaver is how we make our living, but it is not worth throwing your life away, not if you can avoid it."

"Is Blackfoot country the only country that is loaded with beaver?" asked Lazarus.

Amos shook his head. "But it has the most population of beaver, especially at Three Forks," he said. "However it is still not worth getting killed over, there are plenty of places that are teaming with beaver and they are not in Blackfoot country."

"When do we start looking for them?" asked Lazarus.

"Patience lad," said Amos. "It is still summer and too early to trap beaver, so first things first." Amos then turned Medicine Hawk and grinned. "I would like to talk to you about Plain Feather."

9

WINTER TRAPPING SEASON

As the summer of 1810 went by, Amos and Plain Feather were married. The groom offered Chief Medicine Hawk five horses for his daughter's hand in marriage. He planned on going on a horse raiding expedition against the Blackfoot or Lakota, but Lazarus offered his uncle the five horses that Yellow Bull gave him as a gift. At first, Amos refused, but Lazarus insisted.

"Consider it as a token of appreciation of my thanks for bringing me out here and teaching me how to be a trapper," said Lazarus.

Amos beamed at his nephew. Hecouldn't have been more proud of him. "What are you going to use to offer the father of your future bride?" he asked.

"I'm sixteen," scoffed Lazarus. "I am too young to get married."

"Your mum was your age, when she married your da," respond Uncle Amos. "Same as your grandmum."

The youth just shrugged. Marriage was far from his mind. Plus,despite his six foot six inch frame and handsome features, he had always been shy around women and never considered himself handsome by any means. He always thought his two older brothers were the prettiest in the family and wasn't surprised that his brother Paul got married not long after meeting his bride.

"You should consider finding yourself a bride, nephew," said Amos. "It can get very lonely out here."

"I will manage, Uncle," said Lazarus. "Now go take these horses and give them to Medicine Hawk before he changes his mind and decides to give his daughter to someone else."

Amos just laughed as he took the horses. He believed that his nephew truly had the makings to be a mountain man and did not regret bringing him to the frontier.

After Amos and Plain Feather were married, they settled in a brand new lodge that her mother, sister and her brothers wives made for them. Amos gave the lodge that he and Lazarus shared to Lazarus. When the tribe moved to their winter campgrounds in the Wind River Mountains, Lazarus had learned how to set up the tipi and take it down by watching the women do it.

Since it took longer by himself to do it, Plain Feather, her mother, and sister offered a helping hand, in which the Scottish youth was grateful. When Plain Feather suggested to Amos that his nephew find himself a wife, he explained to her that the boy didn't think he was ready for that yet.

"He thinks he is too young and ugly for a woman to be interested in him," said Amos.

Plain Feather at first was in shock, but then laughed. "If he paid attention to how many girls in my village are fighting each other just to be alone with him, he will see how foolish he sounds."

Amos chuckled as he agreed with his bride, but they both decided not to force the issue. Lazarus was more interested in learning to be a trapper like his uncle. There'll be plenty of time for women. As the village settled at the foot of Squaretop Mountain in what is now known as the Bridger Wilderness, Amos and Lazarus along with some warriors, would go hunting to provide meat for the village. Every now and then they would come back with moose, elk, or black bear.

On one occasion, Lazarus encountered his first grizzly bear when it chased Lame Deer up a tree. He managed to shoot the beast in the shoulder, causing it to turn his undivided attention on him. Lazarus managed to lure the grizzly away from his friend while kicking his heels into his horses flanks pushing it to run as fast as it will carry him.

That was long enough for Amos, Running Dog, and the rest of the Crow hunting party to come to the rescue and finish off the beast; firing both muskets and arrows into it until it fell to the earth never to rise again. Lame Deer was grateful for what Lazarus had done, that not only was a feast held in the youth's honor, but Lame Deer gave Lazarus seven horses as a token of his thanks.

Lazarus wanted to refuse, but remembered that to do so, would be an insult. So he not only accepted the gift but told Lame Deer that his friendship was worth just as much as the horses. Amos beamed with pride as he watched his nephew clasped arms with the Crow warrior, forming a bond of friendship.

"He truly has the makings of a mountain man," he said to himself.

As the grizzly bear was skinned and the meat was shared, it was decided that the claws would be shared by Lazarus, Amos, Lame Deer, and Running Dog, while the skin was given to the village medicine man Black Bird as sign of strength. No one disagreed.

During the feast, Amos informed his nephew that they would be leaving soon to find beaver trapping grounds. It was now the second week of September and the winter trapping season would be coming soon.

"Do you know any beaver trapping grounds that are not in Blackfoot country?" asked Lazarus.

Amos smirked. "I know one in a valley north of here," he said. "It is in Flathead country, but that don't mean we won't have any visitors from the Blackfoot."

Lazarus shrugged. "Well whenever you and Plain Feather are ready to leave, I'm right behind you." Amos just nodded as his wife served bear stew to him and Lazarus.

A few days later, the trio left the village of Medicine Hawk and headed north. Plain Feather was riding behind Amos on a spotted mare. She was armed with a Pennsylvania rifle and two flintlock pistols that Amos had given her a year ago, before he left to visit his kin back east.

He taught her how to use it and she was an adept student, often joining her husband and nephew on hunts and was shooting as proficient as they were. Lazarus' lessons never ceased, as he was now learning the Crow tongue while he was in the village. Amos and Plain Feather continued those lessons with him, often speaking to each other in Crow and testing and showing him what plants and animals were said in that language.

Lazarus was enjoying the lessons, however he was having a hard time getting used to Amos and Plain Feather's love making at night. Even though they were in their own lodge and he was in his own lodge, the entire forest could hear them.

One morning, Lazarus was going down by the creek to take a bath and walked right into his uncle and aunt making love in the creek. The sight shocked and scared the youth out of his wits, that as he turned around to run back to camp, he ran right into a tree, knocking himself out in the process. He later woke up inside his lodge with Plain Feather holding a wet cloth over his head to quell the swelling on his nogging, while his uncle was just kneeling over him smirking.

"See anything you liked lad?" Lazarus immediately sat up and then quickly regretted it.

"I'm sorry Uncle Amos and Aunt Plain Feather," he said. "I didn't mean to, I didn't know you two were going to be down there."

"Well shiite nephew we know that," laughed Amos.

"I told you he needs a woman," said Plain Feather in Crow as she chuckled.

Lazarus was quiet for a moment, as he took the cloth from his aunt and gently pressed it on his swollen head.

"You Ok Lazarus?" asked Amos.

"Why do you and Aunt Plain Feather think I need a woman?"

Amos and Plain Feather looked at each other and beamed with pride.

"He has been learning," she said.

"Why do you think ye don't?" asked Amos. "

I wouldn't know what to do with one," said Lazarus. "I have never been with one."

"You mean you're a virgin?"

Lazarus nodded.

"Well, hell, that's nothing to be ashamed of, lad," said Amos. "I didn't get my first kiss until I joined the Army."

"So Aunt Plain Feather is your first?" asked Lazarus.

"I didn't say that now lad," laughed Amos.

Plain Feather was confused, at first, but then she remembered a conversation that she and Amos had on this particular subject and how white people viewed the subject.

"So it is true that you white men believe that sex before marriage is wrong?"

"Most of us do," answered Amos. "But don't always practice what we believe."

Now Lazarus was a little confused.

"Indians don't have sex before marriage?"

"I hear the Cheyennes and the Arapaho don't," answered Amos. "But Lazarus, Indians don't view sex as we whites do."

"Oh," said Lazarus.

"It doesn't make us better than them or them worst than us," said Amos. "They're just different from us, doesn't make them bad people, which is more than I could say for our kind."

"What do you mean?"

"Remember when I first visited you and told your family about Plain Feather?"

Lazarus nodded.

"You remember how your father reacted when he found out that she was not white?" It all became clear to Lazarus.

"I understand now," he said. "Is that why you choose to live out here, despite the dangers?"

"Aye lad," answered Amos. "Indians are more honest. Even those who don't like you, like the Blackfoot, it is not because of skin color but they are trying to protect what is theirs."

"I can respect that," said Lazarus.

Amos patted his nephew on the shoulder.

"Most of our kind don't," he said. "Now get some rest. We continue our journey north tomorrow."

"I have to go down the creek and take a bath," said Lazarus. "That's if you two lovebirds are done using it."

Both Amos and Plain Feather guffawed, as the former slapped his nephew on the back.

The place the trio headed was a valley called Silver Bow Valley, which bordered the Continental Divide, where the city of Butte, Montana now stands. They were going to the Clark Fork River, which was in Flathead country.

Amos had trapped and hunted there on many occasions and had friends among the Flathead tribe, who called themselves the Salish. It would take a couple of days to get there, barring any delays, but Amos knew there would be beaver and would spend the winter trapping season teaching his nephew the trapping trade - with Plain Feather's help of course.

They arrived by the middle of September. They camped not far from the river and, once they set up their lodges, Lazarus volunteered to go hunting. His uncle told him to be wary and watch his topknot.

"My what?"

"Topknot," said Amos. "That means pay attention to your surroundings, because if you don't, you might lose your scalp."

"I will remember that uncle," said Lazarus.

As the youth rode off on his black stallion, pulling a packhorse, Amos took the coffee pot and decided to go down to the river and fill it while checking for beaver lodges. He made sure Plain Feather was Ok by herself for a while. She assured him that she will be fine, showing him her rifle and pistols, all locked and loaded.

Lazarus didn't have to ride far from the camp, before he spotted a bull elk in the distance. Realizing his good fortune, he checked his prime and readied his rifle. The elk was within shooting distance, but had not smelled or spotted him yet. Lazarus aimed at his target, took a breath and fired. He hit his target, but as he fired he frightened his horse, causing him to buck. Buck he did, knocking his rider over.

Lazarus managed to land on his rump while both his horse and pack mule ran to God knows where.

"Bloody Hell!!" he shouted.

It was at that moment he heard giggling from a nearby bush. He managed to stand up and saw two Indian women giggling at him. One appeared to be in her thirties but the other one appeared to be around Lazarus' age and he thought that she was the most beautiful woman he had ever seen.

10

THE WAY YOU MAKE ME FEEL

LAZARUS DIDN'T KNOW whether to run, laugh or say something to the women. The way they were dressed was different from the Crow, so Lazarus knew that they weren't Crow, but he also wasn't sure if they were Blackfoot. Just as he was about to use sign language, three warriors arrived with his missing horse and pack mule.

The women were still giggling as the older one spoke to one of the three warriors. From what Lazarus could gather, he was probably her husband and they were parents of the younger Indian girl, because she looked like both of them. Lazarus decided to take a chance.

"I am a friend," he said in sign. "What tribe are you?"

"Salish," said the man in sign.

He quickly dismounted and approached the youth.

"You white men call us Flathead."

Lazarus nodded, before pointing to his animals. "Those are my horses," he said in sign.

The warrior suddenly smirked. "I know," he said. "My wife and daughter say you fall off one of them after shooting the elk."

The man's wife and daughter continued to laugh, followed by the two other warriors who were holding Lazarus's animals. Before long, the youth laughed along and thanked the man and his warriors for returning his horses.

"My name is," he said in sign, then spoke it through mouth. "Lazarus."

The women and the warriors tried to pronounce his name with great difficulty.

"Lazaaruusss!" said the girl. The youth smiled and nodded his approval.

She smiled back, with her parents looking back and forth between the two suspiciously.

"I have an Indian name," he said in sign. "I am called White Bear by the Omaha and the Crow."

"I am Plenty Hawk," said the warrior. "My wife Fighting Bear Woman and our daughter Dark Wind."

Lazarus doffed his hat and bowed before the ladies who just giggled.

"Why are you in our lands?"

"I came here with my uncle and his wife," answered Lazarus in sign. "They are going to teach me how to be a trapper."

"They should teach you not to fall off horses, when you hunt," signed Dark Wind. Her father grunted at her. Her mother spoke to her in their Salish tongue, causing the young lady to bow her head.

"Who is your uncle?" asked Plenty Hawk in sign.

"White Horse Talker," answered Lazarus. "His white name is Amos Mackinnon."

A look of recognition appeared on Plenty Hawk's face.

"I know him," said Plenty Hawk in sign. "He is an honorable man."

"Thank you."

Plenty Hawk and the two young men, his son Lone Falcon and nephew Shooting Arrow, offered to help Lazarus butcher the elk and take the meat back to his camp. The youth graciously accepted and told the trio that his camp wasn't far.

Fighting Bear Woman and Dark Wind went back to their village, but not before Dark Wind looked over her shoulder and smiled at the young man. Lazarus blushed, but then quickly suppressed his smile when he noticed that Plenty Hawk, Lone Falcon, and Shooting Arrow were noticing the interaction between the two. The trio suddenly chuckled as they helped him with the meat. It was around sunset, Lazarus rode in camp with the elk meat and his new friends.

"About bloody time you showed up," said Amos. "You had us worried sick!"

Amos suddenly recognized Plenty Hawk and his demeaner changed.

"Plenty Hawk is it really you?"

"Shake my hand brother and you will see that I am real," said the Flathead warrior in heavily accented english.

Lazarus was dumbfounded. "If you speak the white man's tongue, why didn't you say something, when we first met?"

"I didn't trust you at first," said Plenty Hawk. "I wanted to know if you are the nephew of Amos MacKinnon."

"Don't hold it against him lad," said Amos. "It is good to see you alive and well my friend."

"And you," said Plenty Hawk. The Flathead warrior turned to Plain Feather and acknowledged her. "Your woman?"

"Well, she is not my nephew's," laughed Amos. Both men laughed as Amos introduced Plain Feather to Plenty Hawk and his son and nephew. "So how did you three run into my nephew here?"

You can ask my mother and sister," said Lone Falcon. "Your nephew has eyes for Dark Wind."

"Now wait a minute," stuttered Lazarus. "I swear it's not what you think it is!"

"And what do you think I think it is?" asked Plenty Hawk. "White Bear Who Falls Off His Horse!"

"Huh?"

"That is the name my daughter has given you," said Plenty Hawk.

"Oh," was all Lazarus could manage. Both Amos and Plain Feather gave Lazarus a wicked grin, as they were putting the meat on the spit.

"You must be mistaken Plenty Hawk," said Amos. "My nephew is more interested in learning how to trap beaver than court women."

"My husband speaks with a straight tongue," said Plain Feather. "White Bear thinks he is too ugly for any woman to be interested in him."

Lazarus turned red, before his uncle and aunt, along with their guests, bursted out laughing.

"Very funny," he said. "I will see to the horses."

The youth took the horses to the river to drink and rubbed them down, while everyone chuckled.

It was apparent that Lazarus had made an impression on Dark Wind. Her father said as much while Amos invited him and his son and nephew to stay the night. Plenty Hawk expressed his gratitude, but since the village was not far from where they were, he invited them to come over and settle for the winter.

There was plenty of game in the valley and it was also loaded with beaver. Amos and Plain Feather thought it over and accepted Plenty Hawk's invitation and gave him and his son and nephew half of the elk meat, as an appreciation for helping Lazarus.

The next morning, Shooting Arrow arrived at their camp to escort them to the village. It didn't take them long to pack up and start traveling. They arrived at the Flathead village about an hour later. The Chief, or leader of the village, was Snake Killer.

He was in his early fifties, but still had the strength and vitality of a much younger man. Shooting Arrow brought the visitors to the Chief to pay their respects. They were greeted by Plenty Hawk, Lone Falcon, and a host of others who sat on the council.

Lone Falcon was twenty years old and already married with a son. Despite his youth, he had counted at least ten coups on his enemies and already owned fifty horses, most of them he captured in horse raiding expeditions against the Blackfoot and Bannock.

Snake Killer invited Amos and Lazarus to smoke the peace pipe. By this time, Lazarus was used to the pipe ceremony, so when it was his turn to smoke, he smoked like a veteran. While he was smoking the pipe, he saw Dark Wind smiling at him, making it hard to concentrate on the smoke. This didn't go unnoticed from Plenty Hawk and Amos and both were chuckling. After the pipe was passed and finished, Chief Snake Killer welcomed Amos and his family.

"It is good to see you again White Horse Talker," he said. "And with a good woman in your life."

"The Creator had blessed me in more ways than one," said Amos. "Now is it just me or are you and your wives getting younger, everytime I see you?"

The Chief and his two wives laughed at the Scotsman's flattery.

"Does your nephew flatter as half as good as you do?" asked Chief Snake Killer in the Flathead tongue.

"I sure hope so," replied Amos. "Plenty Hawk's daughter has eyes on him."

Since Lazarus didn't speak Flathead, he didn't know what was being said. Based on the fingers being pointed at him, and the laughter, he sensed that his uncle and their hosts were talking about him.

"Dark Wind is beautiful isn't she?" Plenty Hawk suddenly asked. Lazarus' mouth just gaped.

"Well just don't sit there you big dummy," said Amos. "Answer the bloody question!"

"Your daughter is very beautiful, Plenty Hawk," Lazarus shyly replied. "Any man would be lucky to have her for a wife."

"I agree," said Plenty Hawk. "Do you wish to court her?"

Again Lazarus's face went blank. He didn't know what to say. In truth, he was smitten with Dark Wind, but he knew nothing about her. He just met her the day before when he looked like a total idiot, at least that is what he thought of himself.

"I don't think your daughter is interested in me," Lazarus finally said. "Especially after how I embarrassed myself in front of her and her mother yesterday."

Chief Snake Killer asked what the youth said and Plenty Hawk translated. The Chief suddenly guffawed, along with everyone else. Then he said something in Flathead and in sign language for the youth's benefit.

"You are not vain White Bear," he said. "This is good."

"Thank you," responded Lazarus. "I think."

"As far as my daughter not being interested in you," said Plenty Hawk. "I will let her be the judge of that."

Plenty Hawk signaled his daughter over and said something to her. She smiled and ran off. A couple of minutes later, she returned with a blanket.

"Looks like she is interested in you lad," said Uncle Amos.

"What is the blanket for?" asked Lazarus.

"You put it over the both of you as your courting," answered Uncle Amos.

"A lot of tribes practice that."

"Really?" said an excited Lazarus. "I mean, wait a minute, I have your permission to court your daughter?"

"You do White Bear Falling Off His Horse," said Plenty Hawk with a laugh.

Lazarus looked to his uncle and aunt for help. "Don't look at us lad," said Uncle Amos. "You heard the man, you have his permission, now shoo!"

Lazarus got up and bowed before Chief Snake Killer and the council and thanked Plenty Hawk for his permission. He took Dark Wind by the hand and as they were walking away from the council, he put the blanket over both of them. Not wanting to look like an idiot, he signed to Dark Wind and asked her where she would like to go. She pointed to a nearby creek and they walked hand in hand under the blanket and sat on the edge of the creek.

Lazarus was in deep thought. He had never been with a woman, never even kissed one and here he was in the mountains courting a pretty Indian woman. The prettiest woman that he ever saw. But why him, he thought to himself.

Lazarus thought there were at least a dozen available and more worthy warriors that would love to court Dark Wind. However, Lazarus remembered something that his grandfather always said. "Never look a gift horse in the mouth." The youth was going to take this opportunity to get to know Dark Wind.

"How old are you Dark Wind?" he asked in sign.

"I have seen sixteen winters," she answered.

"I have seen sixteen winters as well," said Lazarus in sign. He smiled after he made the last statement. "Do you speak the white man's tongue?"

"A little," she said. "Lazaaarruss." The youth chuckled.

"Lazarus Buchanan," he said pointing at himself.

"Lazaarusss Beeeoooouuucanon," she said in pronouncing his full name.

This time he laughed. "That's good," he said in sign. "Do you speak Crow?"

"Some," she said in english. "Do you speak Salish?"

Lazarus frowned and shook his head. "How do you know sign and Crow?"

"My Uncle and Plain Feather teach," he said in sign. "I would like to speak Flathead or Salish."

"I teach you," she said in English.

"You would?" he asked, almost shouting.

She nodded her head and giggled.

"I'm sorry Dark Wind," said Lazarus. "I have never been with a woman."

"You not like women?"

"No I like women very much," said Lazarus. "I don't think that they like me."

"I like you." The youth turned beet red. She had that affect on him and she knew it. He loved it.

"You are very beautiful Dark Wind," he said. "I would love to teach you more of my tongue, if you teach me yours."

Dark Wind smiled and nodded. Lazarus was thanking God that they were sitting down, because his legs were shaking. "Good Lord," he thought to himself. "What is it about this girl that has me weak in the knees?"

Lost in his thoughts, the youth almost jumped as Dark Wind touched his hair. It was a gentle touch, but it felt heavenly, at least according to him.

"You not like my touch?" she asked.

"I like your touch very much," said Lazarus. "Its the way you make me feel."

"How do I make you feel?" Lazarus looked into her eyes and as she looked back, he managed to find the right words.

"Special," he said. "You make me feel special."

Without warning, Lazarus suddenly kissed her. It was his first kiss, apparently it was hers too. Once he stopped, she had a surprised look on her face. Lazarus was about to apologize, but then without warning she kissed him back before he had the chance. Before long they were in a loving embrace, enjoying their first passionate kiss, like a bear that got it's first taste of honey.

11

PLIGHT OF ANDREW HENRY

WHILE LAZARUS CONTINUED to court Dark Wind, it wasn't long before he and his uncle were trapping beaver. Lazarus was an adept student and quickly soaked up the lessons he was learning like a sponge. Before the end of October, he was pulling in as much beaver as his uncle. With her parents' permission, Dark Wind would join Lazarus on his trapping trips with his uncle and aunt and would help them skin and dry the beaver pelts.

The beaver fur was thick and would catch an excellent price in St. Louis. By the middle of November, winter hit with a fury and the trapping season was over. Amos, Plain Feather, and Lazarus had over six hundred beaver plews just from one season. When the weather cleared, Amos planned to cache them, before heading west to the Snake River to explore for more beaver trapping grounds.

They wintered in the village of Snake Killer. During those months, even when they were trapping, Lazarus and Amos would go and hunt to help provide for the village. Despite the weather the forest in the valley was teaming with game.

The duo, along with some warriors, would return with moose and elk. First week of December Amos took Lazarus high up into the mountains to hunt Bighorn sheep. They spent two days up there, but managed to come back with three of them.

As the winter of 1810 turned into 1811 and Lazarus celebrated his seventeenth birthday, his courtship with Dark Wind continued and his feelings for her grew. He would go hunting with her brother to help provide for the family, when the weather permitted, and nine times out of ten they were successful.

Good news arrived in the village when Plain Feather announced that she was pregnant. Both Amos and Lazarus danced a jig in the snow to celebrate. Amos couldn't have been much happier that he was going to be a father for the first time and Lazarus was going to have a cousin.

As winter turned into spring, Amos, Plain Feather, and Lazarus left the village to head west for better trapping grounds. Lazarus promised Dark Wind that he would return before the summer and Amos assured her that he will make sure that his nephew kept that promise.

They cached their plews about two miles from Silver Bow Creek, before heading west, then south. A couple of days later they arrived at what is now known as Henry's Fork, which was a 127 mile tributary of the Snake River, and they found themselves not alone. They found themselves outside a small fort, not far from the river, and it was manned.

"Halt," shouted a man from the walls of the fort.

"Take it easy lad," responded Amos. "We're friends."

Suddenly the door opened and a man that Amos immediately recognized appeared.

"Aren't you a friend of John Colter?" he asked.

"Aye," answered Amos. "Aren't you Andrew Henry?"

The man nodded and immediately approached the trio and shook hands with Amos.

"What the hell are you doing out here?" he asked.

"I could ask you the same question," said Amos. "Aren't you supposed to be at Three Forks?"

"We were at Three Forks," said Andrew Henry. "The blasted Blackfoot chased us out."

"I'm not surprised," said Amos. "This is my wife Plain Feather and my nephew Lazarus."

"Pleasure to make your acquaintance," said Andrew Henry. "Come on inside."

The trio followed the trader and co-owner of the Missouri Fur Company inside. Once inside, Amos and Lazarus counted at least sixty weary souls in this fort, which was dubbed Fort Henry. Everyone sat down, except those on guard duty, while fish was being cooked.

Amos noticed the piles of pelts in the corner. "Looks like things have been profitable for you Mr. Henry," he said.

"A lot of good it will do me and mine if we don't make it back to St. Louis alive," said Henry. "As you can see I had to abandoned Fort Lisa and come over the Divide, it was the only way to save the rest of my men from those devils."

"If you wish, my nephew and I will hunt for you and your men," said Amos. "My woman is a great cook."

"I thank you," said Henry. "How long have you been out here?"

"We left St. Louis in May of last year," answered Amos. "This is my nephew's first winter and spring in the mountains."

"Did you by any chance see John Colter while you were in St. Louis?"

"We did," answered Amos. "We heard what happened to George Drouillard from the Crow last summer."

"I take it that he was a friend of yours too?" asked Henry. Amos nodded.

"I'm sorry," said Henry. "I'm truly sorry."

"Mr. Henry what in the hell where you thinking in going into Three Forks?" asked Amos. "John Colter warned you and Manuel Lisa that the Blackfoot would rather kill you than trade with you."

"I know it," said Andrew Henry. "But Lisa thought that he was a savvy business man and I gave him my word that I will bring back beaver pelts."

"At what cost?" said Lazarus all of sudden. "The Blackfoot consider the beaver sacred, so at what cost?"

"Nine men," said Andrew Henry. "Nine innocent men who were my responsibility."

"What's done is done," said Amos. "No point in beating yourself up over it now." Amos looked around and surveyed the scene. Andrew Henry and his men have obviously been here awhile and have been more successful in trapping here, than at Three Forks.

"So what happens now?"

"We're going to finish trapping this spring," said Andrew Henry. "By summer we head out to St. Louis."

"Could you use some extra guns?" asked Amos.

"You and yours would be welcomed," said Henry.

"We have to stop in Silver Bow Valley to pick up our plews and visit our Flathead friends," said Amos. "We can escort you from there and safety in numbers."

"I would be indebted to you," said Henry.

Amos just nodded. "Lazarus and I are going to go hunt for some game," he said. "Can I trust my wife around your men?"

"I give you my word she will be safe." Amos turned to Plain Feather, who just nodded. She kept her pistols in her belt and in plain sight to the men, that she was not to be trifled with.

"We're also going to explore for better trapping grounds," said Amos. "Will that be a problem?"

"Shouldn't be," said Andrew Henry. "There is plenty of beaver up and down this river for everyone."

Amos nodded. "Let's go nephew."

"Right behind you uncle," said Lazarus as he follow his uncle out of the Fort to hunt.

12

JUST WHEN YOU THOUGHT THAT IT WAS SAFE

DURING THE REST of the spring of 1811, Amos and Lazarus would trap up and down the Snake River, along Henry's Fork and the Teton River, pulling in another 300 beaver plews by the end of the spring. Andrew Henry's men were pulling in their fair share amount of beaver plews as well and there was no conflict between them and Amos, Plain Feather, and Lazarus.

Plain Feather was beginning to show, but not by much, since the baby wasn't due until the fall. Keeping true to their word, the uncle and nephew duo continued to hunt and provide meat for the fort; bringing in elk, moose and on a couple of occasions mountain buffalo - which were a subspecies of the plains buffalo. Sticking to his plan, Andrew Henry and his men left the fort at the beginning of May.

Amos, Plain Feather, and Lazarus lead them north over the Divide. They went towards Silver Bow Valley so they could pick up their cache of plews.When they recovered their plews, Lazarus used the seven horses that Lame Deer gave him as pack animals to help carry their catch of now over 900 beaver plews.

Andrew Henry asked Amos if it was possible, if they could find the Flathead village they wintered with to help trade for horses.

Amos didn't see a problem with that. However they needed to find the village, because the Flatheads were a nomadic tribe.

As they were traveling, they heard gunshots from over a hill. Amos, Lazarus, and Henry went to investigate. When they dismounted, Henry looked through his spyglass and saw a village being attacked by the Blackfoot. He handed the spyglass to Amos, who got a look.

"That's Snake Killer's village," said Amos. "We have to help," said Lazarus.

"That's exactly what we are going to do lad!"

"Just when you thought it was safe," said Andrew Henry. "The Blackfoot got to come and ruin everything."

"This isn't your fight Mr. Henry," said Amos. "Those are our friends down there, you and your men just look after me wife and our plews."

"Like Hell!" shouted Andrew Henry. "My men and I have some scores to settle with the Blackfoot. You two go down there and help your friends and I will regroup with my men and bring some of them to help reinforce you!"

"Thank you," said Amos.

He and Lazarus rode down to the Flathead village to help their friends. True to his word, Andrew Henry rode back to his men and told them the situation. Out of the sixty men, half of them volunteered to join Andrew Henry and help Amos and Lazarus help the Flathead repel the Blackfeet, while the other half volunteered to stay with Plain Feather and watch over the plews.

Snake Killer's village was under attack from their hated enemy the Blackfoot and, as with most battles between enemy tribes, this was extremely personal. Plenty Hawk, his son Lone Falcon, and his nephew Shooting Arrow were among the defenders fiercely fighting off the invaders.

Plenty Hawk took an arrow to his leg, but was not out of the fight. As his son tended to his leg, the War Chief continued to shoot at the Blackfoot invaders with the Kentucky long rifle Amos Mackinnon had given him. Loading and reloading, he never stopped.

Just as Lone Falcon finished wrapping a tourniquet around his father's leg, both he and his father noticed that two Blackfoot warriors coming towards them. A shot rang out and the first, and then second, were shot off their horses. They realized that the shots didn't come from anyone in the village. Suddenly war cries were heard coming from the west, as Amos Mackinnon and Lazarus Buchanan rode in on their stallions with their rifles smoking.

"Saw you from over the horizon," said Amos in Flathead. "Thought you could use some help." "We're indebted to you White Horse Talker," said Plenty Hawk.

"We have more men coming," added Lazarus. As soon as he said that Andrew Henry and his men appeared over the horizon, shouting at the top of their lungs while charging in, guns blazing. Seeing that they have allies, the Flathead defenders managed to mount up and charge against the Blackfoot. They joined Andrew Henry and his men, followed by Amos and Lazarus.

Realizing the tide turned against them, the Blackfoot retreated and headed north back to their own territory. Lazarus was reloading his rifle when a Blackfoot warrior shot his horse out from under him, causing him to fly off it as the animal fell.

Lazarus landed on his side, knocking the wind out of him, but he quickly regained his composure. The Blackfoot warrior was coming straight for him, war club in hand. Without hesitation, Lazarus took out one of his pistols, aimed, and fired. His adversary dropped to the ground, a neat hole between his eyes.

The coalition of Flathead and trappers chased the Blackfoot invaders back to their territory while Lazarus looked around to make sure that there were no more enemy warriors. He quickly reloaded his pistol and Harper's Ferry rifle and by the time he was done, he was greeted by the smiling Shooting Arrow.

"I saw what you did White Bear," said Shooting Arrow in heavily accented english. "You have strong medicine."

"Or dumb luck," said Lazarus.

Shooting Arrow laughed and went to check on the Blackfoot warrior that Lazarus had killed. Suddenly he whooped and cheered to high heaven. Lazarus had a look of confusion on his face as he watched his friend dance in circles around the Blackfoot he just shot. By the time Shooting Arrow was done, the Flathead and trappers had returned from chasing the invaders.

"Do you know who you have killed White Bear?" asked Shooting Arrow.

"No but I have a feeling you're going to tell me," said Lazarus.

"This is Snake In The Grass," said Shooting Arrow. "Among our enemies, he is the worst!"

Shooting Arrow repeated the last statement in Flathead to the warriors and they all whooped and cheered. Amos just sat on his horse and beamed at his nephew. Before Lazarus knew it, all the Flatheads, man, woman, and child came from the village to either pat him on the back or touch him.

Chief Snake Killer and Plenty Hawk, who was leaning on his son, arrived, followed by Dark Wind and Fighting Bear Woman. Shooting Arrow showed the body of Snake In The Grass to everyone and said that he witnessed White Bear killing the people's most hated enemy. Both Chief Snake Killer and Plenty Hawk smiled at Lazarus.

"Your medicine is strong," said Chief Snake Killer as he placed his hands on Lazarus' shoulders.

"I'm glad to have helped," said Lazarus.

Lazarus looked at Dark Wind, who was smiling at him, before turning his attention to Plenty Hawk and his leg.

"You're hurt," he said.

"I am fine White Bear," said Plenty Hawk. "Take care of Snake In The Grass."

"I have already taken care of him," said Lazarus.

"He means take his scalp nephew," said Amos.

A shocked look came over Lazarus' face. Even when he and his uncle fought the Lakota last year, he was able to avoid taking scalps. This would be his first scalp taking.

"Go on nephew," said Amos.

Lazarus looked at the village and saw everyone expecting him to take the scalp of the hated Blackfoot warrior Snake In The Grass. He just nodded and walked to the body and, with a little hesitation, managed to take his scalp. When all was said and done, the entire village whooped and cheered.

Amos smiled at his nephew and said "You truly have the makings of a mountain man."

Amos Mackinnon, Andrew Henry, and the rest of the trappers returned to the trapping party and Plain Feather while Lazarus stayed behind with the villagers and his new celebrity status. Amos told Plain Feather what Lazarus did and to say she was thrilled was an understatement.

Apparently, the Blackfoot warrior was a bain on the Crow just as much as it was on the Flathead. The entire trapping party returned to the village of Snake Killer, where Snake In The Grass's body was mutilated by the women. Those Flathead defenders who were killed in the attack by the Blackfoot, were buried and mourned by their loved ones.

Plenty Hawk, and others who were wounded, had their wounds tended. Lazarus went to check on Plenty Hawk to see how he was doing and the War Chief assured him that the leg wound was not serious and had given the youth his permission to continue his courtship with his daughter.

After the dead were buried and mourned, a feast was held in honor of Andrew Henry and his men for coming to the aid of the Flathead village. Henry and his men were grateful. Amos, on behalf of Henry, asked Chief Snake Killer if there is any possibility they could trade for horses for transportation of their beaver plews.

The Chief discussed this request with the council and everyone agreed that since Andrew Henry, along with Amos Mackinnon and his nephew, helped defend the village from their hated enemy and since Lazarus killed Snake In The Grass, the least they could do is help them with horses.

The council told Amos Mackinnon to inform Andrew Henry to pick as many horses as he needed. Amos told Andrew Henry the good news and to say that the trader was relieved was an understatement.

13

FACE OF THE SUN

ANDREW HENRY and his men stayed in the village for a couple of days. That was enough time to get the amount of horses they needed to carry the rest of their pelts. Amos managed to negotiate and translate between them and Chief Snake Killer and everything ended amicably.

Lazarus spent most of his time with Dark Wind, learning the Flathead tongue from her while she improved her English. He knew before long that he would have to travel with his uncle and aunt, to escort Andrew Henry and his men back to St. Louis. Lazarus promised Dark Wind that he would return to her as soon as possible and, when he did, he was going to ask her father for her hand in marriage. He approached the subject with his uncle and aunt, who were walking by the creek together.

"There is something I should tell you," he said. Amos and Plain Feather looked at their nephew with anticipation. "When we return, I am going to ask Plenty Hawk for Dark Wind's hand in marriage."

"Well it's about bloody time," shouted Amos.

He attempted to give his nephew a bear hug, but the youth was too big and too tall. Plain Feather giggled at the antics of her husband and nephew.

"When will you ask Plenty Hawk for his daughter's hand in marriage?"

"When we return from St. Louis and resupply ourselves for the next two seasons," answered Lazarus.

"Plain Feather won't be accompanying us to St. Louis," said Amos. "We talked about it, she wants to stay with her people, until we return."

"Will we be back in time before the baby is born?" asked Lazarus.

Amos nodded. "If we leave tomorrow and, barring any delays, we should be back before the fall trapping season."

The next day Amos, Plain Feather, and Lazarus led Andrew Henry and his caravan out of Snake Killer's village. Before they left, Lazarus again promised Dark Wind that he will return and informed her father and brother that he wanted to discuss something important.

Plenty Hawk and Lone Falcon assured him that they will be here waiting, before seeing him off. The caravan traveled up Clark's Fork to the Yellowstone River before following it south to the northern Little Bighorn River.

They found the Crow village of Medicine Hawk and stayed with them for a couple of days. The Crow Chief and his wife, Blue Willow, were happy that they were about to become grandparents and assured Amos that their daughter and future grandchild were safe with them and among the people while he and Lazarus traveled down the Yellowstone to find Manuel Lisa.

They traveled up the Yellowstone River to the mouth of the Missouri River and followed it down to the Heart River, where Bismarck, North Dakota, now stands. It was there they found Manuel Lisa at his fort, called Fort Manuel.

The Spaniard was planning to return to Three Forks to search for Andrew Henry, but was surprised and relieved to see him return alive and well and with pelts.

"Senor Henry," he shouted. "I am happy to see that you are alive and well!"

"I have your pelts Manuel," said Andrew Henry even handedly.

He slowly got down from his horse and went to his pack animals. Some of the beaver plews or pelts that were trapped at Three Forks, he threw them down at Manuel Lisa's feet.

"George Drouillard trapped those before the Blackfoot beheaded him last year," he said. "Three more of my men managed to trap these before they lost their lives at the hands of the Blackfoot."

Amos and Lazarus sat on their horses and listened to the exchange between the two partners.

"I lost a total of nine men," said Andrew Henry. "Nine innocent souls, whose bodies are bleached at Three Forks by the face of the sun."

"But you have survived Senor Henry," said Manuel Lisa.

"My men and I barely survived," responded Andrew Henry. "Had it not been for Amos Mackinnon, and his nephew Lazarus Buchanan, our bodies would still be up there over the Divide and being bleached by the face of the sun."

"Either way I am grateful for you," said Manuel Lisa.

"Don't be," responded Andrew Henry. "May God forgive me for what I have done."

Amos and Lazarus decided that they were not going to sell their plews to Manuel Lisa, not after the exchange between him and Henry. They spent the night at Fort Manuel before leaving the next morning and traveling down the Missouri towards St. Louis.

It was already the middle of June, they guessed they'd reach St. Louis by the first or second week of July. Lazarus had learned a lot over the passed year and now, at seventeen, he had already built a reputation as a successful trapper, like his uncle, and more. He had become a warrior fighting against both the Lakota and the Blackfoot.

He and his uncle helped Andrew Henry and his surviving trapping party to find their way back to Manuel Lisa and avoid any further entanglements with the Blackfoot. He was wooing a Flathead girl that he intended to marry. Life was good.

He just prayed that he lived long enough to enjoy it and learn from not just his mistakes, but the mistakes of others, so his body won't end up like so many others who foolishly tread into Three Forks or other Blackfoot territory to trap beaver.

Lazarus learned that the frontier showed no mercy to fools and idiots and he would be damned if his body was going to be bleached in the mountains or on the prairie by the face of the sun because of foolishness.

"Why don't we sell our plew to Manuel Lisa, Uncle?" asked Lazarus.

"I don't like him," answered Amos. "It's a matter of principle to me, I mean John Colter warned him that to go into Three Forks was suicide and he still sent Andrew Henry there."

Amos paused for a moment as he was pulling his string of pack horses. "Never trust a man like that nephew," he said. "Men like that are the most dangerous kind of fools."

"I will remember," said Lazarus.

"Good."

14

SECOND WINTER

THEY ARRIVED IN ST. Louis by the middle of July. While Amos and Lazarus didn't sell their 900 hundred beaver plews to Manuel Lisa, they did sell them to one of his partners: Auguste Pierre Chouteau, who had his own financial problems last year when his trading post among the Mandan Indians was destroyed by a fire, losing all the beaver pelts he acquired.

He gave Amos and Lazarus a generous price for their beaver plews, since they were in supreme condition, at $10 per plew. The duo fared better than Chouteau's partners Manuel Lisa and Andrew Henry and, as a result, the Missouri Fur Company did not make a successful profit during it's first three years in existence.

After getting paid a total of $9,000, the uncle and nephew duo went to resupply themselves for the next two trapping seasons. They mostly bought guns to trade with the Crow, Flathead, and other friendly tribes, but also trapping supplies and ammunition; before buying coffee, sugar, food, and foofaraw for Plain Feather, Dark Wind and their families.

By the time the duo was done with their shopping there remained over $5,000 cash, so they split it between them and deposited it in a bank account that Amos had already opened when he started his trapping career. He helped Lazarus create his own bank account and deposit his money in it.

Afterwards they went to visit John Colter, who was now married to a beautiful woman named Sallie and was expecting a baby soon. The duo not only visited the legend, but were surprised to see another legend, who lived not far from Colter. This was none other than Daniel Boone. The seventy-six old frontiersman often visited the Colter residence during his walks and came to meet Amos Mackinnon and Lazarus Buchanan, while walking his dog. He regaled the uncle and nephew duo, along with Colter, of his adventures.

After staying with Colter and his growing family for a couple of days, Amos and Lazarus left St. Louis and traveled back to the Rocky Mountains. Amos planned to arrive among the Crow village of Medicine Hawk by late September, or the first week of October.

He hoped to get there before the baby arrived. They traveled twenty to thirty miles a day, following the Missouri River. They managed to reach the Omaha village of Yellow Bull by the third week of August. They stayed with him for a couple of days, trading some of the guns for more horses, before continuing their journey to the Yellowstone River.

By mid September they reached the Crow Village of Medicine Hawk. Plain Feather was ecstatic to see her husband and nephew safely returned to her and just in time. A few days later after they returned, she went into labor and gave birth to a healthy baby boy.

Amos named his new son, Angus, after his father and his Crow name would be White Cloud. Lazarus was happy for his uncle and aunt and welcomed his new baby cousin, cradling the little infant in his arms. Lazarus noticed the baby had blue eyes, like his father, and while he could pass for a full blooded Crow Indian,Lazarus noticed that his new cousin looked alot like his namesake; Grandda Angus Mackinnon. That's when Lazarus made a decision.

"I will be leaving in a couple days," he said. "But I will be back in time for the winter trapping season."

"And just where do you think you're going?" asked Uncle Amos.

"To find Chief Snake Killer's village," answered Lazarus. "I'm going to ask Dark Wind to marry me."

Both Amos and Plain Feather beamed with pride. "She will make you a fine wife nephew," said Plain Feather. "But you shouldn't go by yourself."

"She is right lad," added Amos. "Give us a couple of days, and we will go with you."

But Lazarus shook his head. "You're needed here Uncle Amos, besides this is something I have to do alone."

"Alone you will get yourself killed," said Uncle Amos.

However, Plain Feather defended her nephew. "You should have better faith in him than that husband," she said. "You taught him everything he knows."

"I also promised his mother that I would look out for him."

"And you have fulfilled your promise Uncle Amos," said Lazarus. "But I am a man now, and this is something I need to do alone."

Amos was in thought for a moment. While it was still September, winter could come at any time, but his nephew was no longer a greenhorn and he had fought and killed enemies of both the Crow and Flathead. He also had successfully trapped beaver, learning his lessons well. In other words the youth proved himself.

"This is going against my better judgement," he said. "But if you are going into Flathead country by yourself, you are not leaving without some supplies and traps."

"I will take only what I need," said Lazarus.

Amos nodded.

A few days later, Lazarus was on the trail. He had his seven pack horses laden with supplies and gifts. Clark's Fork River was just a few days west from Medicine Hawk's village, but Lazarus was in no rush. Before he left, it was agreed that they would meet up at Clark's Fork River for the winter trapping season.

Plain Feather planned to help her village move to the their winter camp in the Wind River Mountains. When Lazarus would camp, he would hobble his animals, unloading each of them and rubbed them down, before feasting on jerky and drinking water. He didn't really care much for coffee, despite that he had sugar, but he remembered that Dark Wind's brother Lone Falcon had a taste for it with or without sugar.

Rarely did he hunt. When he did, he usually went after small game, like rabbits and quail. He was always alert, as his uncle taught him. Grizzly bears were still on the prowl, fattening themselves up for winter, and he didn't want to have an encounter with one. Especially since he was alone in the mountains.

He managed to find Chief Snake Killer's village at the end of September in Silver Bow Valley. The village welcomed him as he rode straight to the Chief's lodge to pay his respects.

"Welcome White Bear," said Chief Snake Killer. "It is good to see you again."

"It is good to be back among the people, Chief Snake Killer," said Lazarus in Flathead.

The white youth hugged the Chief and informed him that his uncle and his aunt just became proud parents. "This is good," said Chief Snake Killer.

"White Horse Talker and Plain Feather will meet me here next moon," said Lazarus. "They send you their love."

Chief Snake Killer nodded with a smile. Before Lazarus had the chance to ask about Dark Wind and her family, her father and brother appeared through the crowd.

"Welcome White Bear," said Plenty Hawk. "It is good have you here safe among us again."

"I'm honored to be here Plenty Hawk," said Lazarus. "I have gifts for you, your family, and Chief Snake Killer."

Lazarus saw Dark Wind and her mother Fighting Bear Woman in the crowd.

"I have something to ask you Plenty Hawk."

"That is?"

"I wish to marry Dark Wind," said Lazarus. "That's if she is willing to be my bride."

Before her father could answer, Dark Wind came from behind him and said, "I wish it!"

Her acknowledgement, caused laughter among the crowd, but no one disapproved of the relationship.

"What do you have to offer for my daughter's hand in marriage?" asked Plenty Hawk. "I have seven horses that I use as pack animals and ten rifles," answered Lazarus.

"I will take five horses and three rifles," said Plenty Hawk.

"Done," said Lazarus. "Come and inspect my animals and my rifles."

After Plenty Hawk was satisfied with the animals and the weapons that Lazarus brought, he nodded his approval and gave his blessing for the youth to marry his daughter. Lazarus and Dark Wind were married according to Flathead custom and the ceremony took place the next day.

Lazarus decided to live in the village with his new bride, taking her on his trapping trips to trap beaver. This turned out to be the best time of his life. Dark Wind was a dutiful bride taking care of her man, and Lazarus had become a loving, dutiful, and caring husband.

When they weren't trapping or hunting, they would be making love, which Lazarus found to be extremely enjoyable. Other than that, Lazarus continued his language lessons with Dark Wind and was impressed that her English was getting better than his Flathead.

He often wished that he could be better at her tongue as she was at his, and he told her as much, but she continued to love him, no more, no less. Uncle Amos and Aunt Plain Feather arrived during the middle of October, trapping beaver on the way.

After paying their respects to Chief Snake Killer and the council, they showed off their baby boy Angus White Cloud. Dark Wind's heart melted, as she looked at her husband's newborn cousin.

"I want to give you a son," she said all of a sudden.

Lazarus beamed at her. "There'll be plenty of time for that, my love," he said in Flathead. With the family reunited, Lazarus's second winter was turning out to be great.

15

THE BLACKFEET

As September rolled into October, Lazarus, Uncle Amos, along with their wives, set out to trap. At first they trapped Clark's Fork River before moving north to the Yellowstone River and heading south again to trap the Little Bighorn River.

Wanting to trap as many beavers as possible, but also avoid the Blackfoot, they stayed and traveled on the Yellowstone, trapping the Tongue and Powder River. They brought in many beaver and had the women skin and dry the pelts while they cooked the meat. Beaver tail was a delicacy among the trappers and nothing was wasted.

They continued to trap up and down the Yellowstone River until the middle of November when winter finally hit with all its fury. They weren't far from Plain Feather's people, so instead of returning to the Flathead, they went and sought out Chief Medicine Hawk's village.

The village was once again staying in the Wind River Mountains, near Stone Top Mountain. It was good to have someone to spend the winter and share the lodge with, so Lazarus thought. He was enjoying married life almost as much as his uncle.

As the winter of 1811 turned into 1812, Lazarus turned eighteen. He could speak both the Crow and Flathead tongue fluently, thanks to Plain Feather, Dark Wind and Uncle Amos. Both he and his Uncle taught their wives not only to speak English better, but also Gaelic, which Amos spoke fluently.

Lazarus' Gaelic was rusty, but as he relearned the language of his parents he was happy to share it with Dark Wind. On the first day of spring in the month of March, Lazarus and Dark Wind decided to go hunting together. She wanted to help provide for the Crow village of Medicine Hawk, who treated her with great kindness. Lazarus had no objection whatsoever.

"You two watch your top knot," said Uncle Amos. "The Blackfoot could be on the prowl, now that winter is over."

"We will Uncle," assured Lazarus. "Don't you worry."

Dark Wind had a brand new Kentucky long rifle that Lazarus bought for her in St. Louis last summer. Since then he taught her how to use and reload it and she was an adept student. However, she also brought her bow and arrow for backup.

They traveled north by northwest to where the Yellowstone emptied into the Powder River. Heeding the advice of his uncle and John Colter, Lazarus avoided going into Blackfoot country. Dark Wind told him that there would be better beaver trapping grounds near the Musselshell River and better hunting as well, but she admitted that while it is Crow country, the Blackfoot have often hunted buffalo there. Lazarus wanted to avoid the Blackfoot at all costs, but at the same time the village needed meat.

"Do you know any place that has better game?" he asked his wife.

"The Little Belt Mountains, where the Musselshell River has forks that rise," she said. "There is buffalo, deer, and elk."

"Have you been there?"

"I have."

"Lead the way then."

They traveled further west from the Yellowstone River towards the Musselshell River. It took them a couple of days to get to the Little Belt Mountains, but once Dark Wind showed that they were at the right place, they immediately set up camp.

While it was late in the day to hunt, both Lazarus and Dark Wind had developed a taste for fish. Once camp was set up and the horses were hobbled, Lazarus went down to the edge of the Musselshell River and fished for their dinner.

While he was down there, Dark Wind sensed something was wrong as if she and her husband were being watched. Suddenly the horses were getting a little jumpy, before she could go to calm them down, three men appeared out of the forest, wearing war paint.

Dark Wind immediately screamed and tried to pull out one of her pistols, but she didn't notice the five other men sneaking up behind her. They immediately grabbed her, but not before she let out another blood curdling scream. Her screams were heard, because Lazarus came in just in time and fired one of his pistols at the feet of one of his wife's abductors.

"Let her go!" he shouted in english.

He didn't know if these warriors understood English or not, but he didn't care. Dark Wind's safety was all that mattered now.

"I said LET HER GO!"

While the warriors obviously didn't speak English they understood the white man's meaning when he had his remaining pistol and Harper's Ferry rifle on them. The five warriors that jumped Dark Wind, immediately released her, but were soon smiling at Lazarus. Dark Wind's facial expression quickly turned to horror.

"Lazarus behind you!" Lazarus quickly turned his head, but was not fast enough as a war club connected to his temple. It didn't do any serious damage, but it was enough to knock him unconscious. Dark Wind screamed and ran to her husband, shaking him to wake up.

"He is not dead Flathead woman," said one of warriors in english. "Not yet anyway."

"You speak the white man's tongue," said Dark Wind.

"Some," said the warrior. "We take you and your man back to our village, where our council will decide how he will die and you will live as my woman."

"I would rather die before I let any of you Blackfoot dogs touch me," said Dark Wind.

The Blackfoot warrior laughed and repeated her statement, causing all the other warriors to laugh.

"That can be arranged," said the Blackfoot warrior, who was obviously the leader of this raiding party. "But first, your man will die."

Lazarus suddenly awoke. Dark Wind tried to help him.

"Easy my husband," she said. "Save your strength."

"I would listen to my woman if I was you," said the Blackfoot warrior.

"Who are you?" asked a groggy Lazarus.

"They are Blackfoot," said Dark Wind.

A look of concern, appeared on Lazarus's face. "What is your name?" he asked the leader that spoke english.

"In your tongue, I am called Black Thunder."

"My wife and I have no quarrel with the Blackfoot," said Lazarus in both english and sign. "Let us go in peace, and there will be no trouble."

"And if we don't let you go in peace?" said Black Thunder with a smirk.

"My uncle is adopted Crow and a friend of the Flatheads," answered Lazarus. "Harm us and the Crow and Flathead will bring merciless vengeance upon you and your people."

Black Thunder saw sheer defiance and courage in the eyes of Lazarus. He believed the white man spoke with a straight tongue.

"You have strength white man," said Black Thunder. "Who is your uncle that lives among the Crow and is a friend to the Flathead?"

"White Horse Talker," answered Lazarus. A look of recognition appeared on the face on Black Thunder. He had obviously heard of Amos MacKinnon.

"And your name?"

"I am called White Bear," answered Lazarus. "Of The village of Chief Snake Killer."

"You killed Snake In The Grass," nodded a coy Black Thunder.

Once he realized that the Blackfoot knew who he was, Lazarus knew that he and his wife were not going to be let go in peace.

"I killed him in battle," he said. "He and his warriors attacked my wife's people."

"I know," said Black Thunder. "I was there."

Lazarus's stomach was churning in fear, but not for himself, for Dark Wind.

"Was he a relative of your's?"

"Does it matter?" asked Black Thunder.

"I guess it doesn't."

"We take you and your women now, back to our village," said Black Thunder. "There the council will decide how you should die."

"Let my wife go," pleaded Lazarus. "She has committed no wrong against you."

"She is an enemy from an enemy tribe," said Black Thunder. "That is enough, but don't worry yourself over her, we will let her live for now."

Black Thunder ordered his warriors to tie their prisoners. Bad news was they were going to kill Lazarus, but the good news was they weren't going to kill him or Dark Wind right there. The fact that the war party was taking the couple back to their village bought them some time.

"Don't worry," said Lazarus in Flathead. "First chance we get, we escape, or die trying."

"I will not let them take me, if they kill you, "responded Dark Wind in Flathead.

"Don't worry," said Lazarus. "We're not dead yet."

"Enough," shouted Black Thunder in english. "I may not speak Flathead, but do not think me a fool." He ordered the couple be separated, so they couldn't plot or plan an escape.

The Blackfoot were the most feared tribe of the northern plains. Their territories ranged from the North Saskatchewan River in what is now Edmonton, Alberta, Canada, to the Yellowstone River of Montana in the United States.

They were a Confederacy consisting of three clans: The Piikani(Piegan), Siksika(Blackfoot Proper), and Kainai(Bloods). They were also allies of the Atsina, who were called Gros Ventre by the trappers. The clan that Black Thunder and his warriors belonged to were the Siksika and were taking Lazarus and Dark Wind to their village, near the Smith River.

The Blackfoot Confederacy were enemies to the Crow, Flathead, Nez Perce, Assiniboine, Lakota, Shoshone, Ute, Cheyenne, Arapaho, Cree, and Ojibwe. Realizing that he had the white man who killed his friend Snake In The Grass, Black Thunder hoped that the council would grant him the honor of avenging his friend's death.

He sensed that the white man called White Bear was an honorable man and since he saw his friend Snake In The Grass die an honorable death in battle. His killer should be given an honorable death. However Black Thunder knew that Lazarus Buchanan and his Flathead woman were in no hurry to greet death.

"Such a pity," he thought to himself. "That Flathead woman would make a fine wife to warm my buffalo robes at night."

16

A NEW FRIEND

AMOS AND PLAIN Feather sensed that something was wrong. Lazarus and Dark Wind had been gone for over a week now and should have been back. Amos sought out his in-laws for help to start a search party. Lame Deer was the first to volunteer in the search. Amos appreciated it.

"We will search the Musselshell River," said Running Dog. "That is where they said they were going, am I right White Horse Talker?"

"You are right," answered Amos.

Plain Feather assured her husband not to fret too much. "Lazarus and Dark Wind can take care of themselves," she said. "You shouldn't worry too much."

"I know," said Amos. "But I knew a lot of men who could take care of themselves and they are no longer alive."

Amos kissed his wife and gave his infant son a peck on the forehead before he, Running Dog, Lame Deer, and the rest of the search party mounted their horses and rode out of the village. Plain Feather and her parents quietly said a prayer to the Creator for their safe return.

Meanwhile, Black Thunder and his warriors arrived with their two captives at their village on the Smith River. The Smith River was a tributary of the Missouri River and flowed northwest in a valley between the Big Belt and Little Belt Mountains.

Lazarus and Dark Wind were taken down from their horses and were brought to the center of the village. Lazarus looked around, seeing mostly hostile faces from men, women, and even children. This gave him a bad feeling, but he showed no fear and neither did Dark Wind.

Exiting his tipi was the leader of the village. His name was Spotted Shield. He was in his early sixties, but still had the strength and vitality of a much younger man. He was also Black Thunder's father. The Chief welcomed his son and his warriors home and inquired about the prisoners.

"My father," said Black Thunder. "My people, this white man is White Bear, the one who took the life of our brother Snake In The Grass, last summer in the land of the Flatheads."

The crowd gave even more hostile looks towards Lazarus and Dark Wind. However, Spotted Shield remained silent, his facial expression was stoic.

"There is more," said Black Thunder. "He is the nephew of the trapper White Horse Thunder, who lives among our enemy the Crow."

"You and your warriors have done well my son," said Spotted Shield. "But I am surprised that you have let an enemy such as this live."

"This enemy is an honorable man, my father," said Black Thunder. "He killed Snake In The Grass in battle, so as such he should die an honorable death and I wish to leave that decision to you and the council."

Chief Spotted Shield smiled for the first time at his son and nodded his approval, as did those who sat on the council. Lazarus did not know what was being said, but something inside was telling him to speak up, so he did.

"I wish to speak," he said. This brought a surprise reaction from the crowd, including Black Thunder.

"Do not beg White Bear," said Black Thunder in english. "You will only dishonor yourself and your woman."

"Tell me Black Thunder," responded Lazarus. "Is it dishonor for a man to plead not just for his own life, but also for the life of the woman he loves?"

Both Black Thunder and Chief Spotted Shield, who knew and spoke some English, looked at the white youth with awe, after he asked his last question.

"Untie him and let him speak," said Chief Spotted Shield.

Black Thunder had one of his warriors cut Lazarus's bonds. With his bonds free, Lazarus started conversing in sign language.

"I am White Bear of the Flathead," he said. "This is my woman Dark Wind and we have no quarrel with the Blackfoot or their allies."

"Did you or did you not kill Snake In The Grass?" asked Chief Spotted Shield in both english and sign.

"I did," responded Lazarus. "And I took his scalp, but it was in battle and he tried to kill me and would have done the same to me."

This quieted the already hostile crowd, some even nodding their heads in agreement. "Also," said Lazarus. "Your warriors attacked the Flathead village that my wife belongs to, my uncle and I were only defending them from your attack. Black Thunder said he was there and saw me kill Snake In The Grass, so he knows I speak with a straight tongue."

Suddenly everyone had their attention on Black Thunder, who nodded. "He speaks with a straight tongue," he said. "Everything this trapper says is exactly the way it happened."

"I know that the flattail is sacred to you and your people," said Lazarus in sign. "My Uncle White Horse Talker and I refuse to tread into your lands and trap the flattail out of respect for your beliefs and tradition."

Chief Spotted Shield and some of the members of the council looked approvingly at Lazarus, after his last statement.

"What are we to do with you White Bear?" asked Chief Spotted Shield. "There are those among us, who wish to kill you, but I cannot help but respect and like you."

Lazarus smiled for a minute.

"You admit to taking Snake In The Grass's scalp?" asked Black Thunder.

Lazarus nodded.

"Do you still have it?"

"I do," replied Lazarus. "But not here, I left it with my other belongings in the Crow village where my wife and I wintered."

Lazarus could see some of the hostility return on some of the faces of the crowd, but not as much as before when he and Dark Wind first arrived.

"As I mentioned I did not want to kill him, but he left me no choice and you know that he would have done the same to me."

"This is true," responded Chief Spotted Shield.

"Are you the leader of this village?" asked Lazarus in sign.

"I am," answered Chief Spotted Shield. "I am called Spotted Shield in your tongue."

"As I mentioned," said Lazarus. "My wife and I have no quarrel with your people, I would like to smoke the peace pipe with you and your warriors and let us return home to our people."

"I would like to do that as well White Bear, but I am afraid that would be impossible."

"Why?"

"By your own words, you are no longer a white man, but a Flat-head and you are friends with the Crow and those two tribes are our enemies," answered Chief Spotted Shield. "We kill our enemies."

"Plus you admitted to killing Snake In The Grass," added Black Thunder. "That cannot go unpunished."

"Then let my wife go," pleaded Lazarus. "She has done no wrong against you."

Again both Chief Spotted Shield and his son, along with those on the council, were impressed with Lazarus. It was clear that this white man did not care what happened to him, his main concern was for his wife.

"You truly love her," said Black Thunder. "Don't you?"

Lazarus looked at Dark Wind, who by this time had a tear

running down her cheek, but she remained steadfast in her defiance against the Blackfoot.

"I love her with all my heart," he said. "I would give my life for her, so that she could live and live free."

"She will live," said Black Thunder. "But as my woman."

"I would rather die, before I let you or any of your dogs touch me," said Dark Wind.

Both Chief Spotted Shield and his son chuckled and looked at Dark Wind with some respect.

"Your woman has spirit," said Chief Spotted Shield.

"I like that," added Black Thunder.

"Is there anyway I can convince you and your people to let her go?" asked Lazarus.

"No," said Black Thunder. "You have my word that she will be decently treated and allowed to mourn your death, after a period of time."

Black Thunder suddenly called out three women from the crowd. He had them take Dark Wind to his lodge, but she refused to be taken without a fight. When Lazarus saw the women trying to drag his wife away, he went into a rage.

"Don't you touch her!!" he shouted and was about to come to his bride's rescue, but was overtaken by ten of Black Thunder's warriors, who pinned the large youth to the ground, but with great difficulty.

"Dark Wind," he shouted. Calling her name over and over again, until Black Thunder knocked him out with a war club.

"Tie him up and take him away," he said. "Was that really necessary my son?" asked Chief Spotted Shield.

"It was father," answered Black Thunder. "We can't risk him and his woman plotting to escape."

"I have never met a white man care so much deeply for a red woman," said a village elder, who appeared to be the same age as Chief Spotted Shield. "I may have misjudged him."

"Doesn't change the fact that he killed your son, Rain In The Face," said Black Thunder.

"No it does not, but at least my son died in battle and like a warrior," responded Rain In The Face. "It is only fitting that the man who took his life should die an honorable death as well."

Everyone agreed as the council followed Chief Spotted Shield and Black Thunder to the council lodge to discuss how Lazarus Buchanan, also known as White Bear, should meet his end.

Little did any of the Blackfoot villagers know there was a woman among them who was secretly plotting to help the captives escape. Her name was Mountain Flower and she was Nez Perce. She was taken from her people almost two years ago and she had lived as a slave with none other than the family of Snake In The Grass.

It was Snake In The Grass who killed Mountain Flower's betrothed and her father during a raid. While Rain In The Face and his wife Sitting Deer treated her kindly, their son was another matter. Snake In The Grass had repeatedly raped her and sometimes would beat her for minor infractions.

When she heard that her abductor met his end at the hands of a white trapper living among the Flathead, she was relieved. Despite the fact that she wanted to escape and return home to her people, fear of what Snake In The Grass' parents and the Blackfoot, would do kept her in line.

Despite that the former continued to treat her kindly, it was no secret that she was still a slave to the enemy of her people. After seeing the man who killed her abductor, Mountain Flower took this as a sign that she must help him and his woman escape, no matter what the cost.

The village of Spotted Shield trusted Mountain Flower enough to walk around without an escort, and she managed to get permission from the elders to bring food to the prisoners.

She first went to Black Thunder's lodge, where Dark Wind was being held. After informing his three wives, who were outside tanning a buffalo hide, that she was there to feed the prisoner she was allowed to go in without second thought.

Dark Wind was tied to a pole in the middle of the lodge, trying to bite through the rawhide that bound her wrists together. Mountain Flower immediately went to her and put the food by her side. Dark

Wind looked at her for a moment and could tell that she was no Blackfoot. Mountain Flower looked at the entrance to make sure that no one was watching.

"You must eat," she signed. "I will help you and your man escape, be patient."

Dark Wind looked at her and nodded. She didn't know how this woman was going to help her escape, but she thought she could trust her.

"I will go to your man and tell him," signed Mountain Flower. "Do you understand?"

Dark Wind nodded. She was able to drink from the bowl of buffalo stew while her hands were still tied. Mountain Flower again assured her that all will be well and to have patience.

After she left the lodge of Black Thunder, Mountain Flower went to where Lazarus was being held. Again she was allowed to go in and feed the prisoner. No one would suspect otherwise. Lazarus sat with his arms tied in front. He was able to rub his noggin, which was hurting from the blow Black Thunder gave him.

When he looked up and saw Mountain Flower, holding what appeared to be a bowl, he held out his hands. She gave it to him and he nodded his thanks and drank and ate from the buffalo stew. Mountain Flower looked out at the entrance to make sure that they were not being watched.

"I am a friend," she said in sign. "I will help you and your woman escape."

She had Lazarus's undivided attention. "Eat as much as you can," she said. You will need your strength."

Lazarus nodded and quietly said "Thank you" in English.

Mountain Flower did not speak the white man's tongue, but she got the jist of what this big white man had said. After eating and drinking the entire bowl, Lazarus handed it back to her. He didn't ask when she would return to help him and Dark Wind escape, but he said a silent prayer that she would and that this would not be his last day or night on earth.

17

ESCAPE AT ALL COST

THE CROW SEARCH party arrived near the Musselshell River. They searched the perimeter to see where Lazarus and Dark Wind camped. Lame Deer found tracks at what looked like to be remnants of a camp. The party came to this location when he called out. As Lame Deer studied the tracks, Amos found something shiny not far from him. It was a crucifix, but any crucifix, it was his nephew's. Lazarus always wore it and rarely took it off.

"They were here," he said.

Lame Deer nodded. "From what I could gather, there was a scuffle."

Running Dog managed to find the tracks and who made them. "Blackfoot," he said. "They lead northwest."

A look of anger and sadness came upon Amos's face. "I told him to be careful," he said.

"Calm yourself White Horse Talker," said Running Dog. "There is no sign of blood or bodies, meaning both White Bear and Dark Wind are possibly still alive."

Amos nodded and hoped that his brother-in-law was right. But God have mercy on those bastards, if they harmed a hair on his nephew and his wife.

At the village of Spotted Shield, the council decided that Lazarus will have a chance to live. In fact, it would be fun for them. They decided the next morning they would strip him naked and make him run. All he has to do is outrun them.

If he succeeds, he will live, but if he doesn't, he will die. Black Thunder went to inform his prisoner of the council's decision and Lazarus was not entirely relieved, but was still a little hopeful. He knew only one man had escaped the Blackoot at this kind of game, but his mind was on Dark Wind.

"I'm not leaving my wife," he said defiantly to Black Thunder.

"I'm afraid you have no choice in the matter," responded the Blackfoot warrior. "We are giving you a chance to live, I would take that chance if I was you and forget about your woman."

"Then you better pray I don't make it," said Lazarus.

Black Thunder was looking at Lazarus with renewed curiosity, when his father entered the lodge. He informed him about their prisoner's concern for his woman, which piqued Chief Spotted Shield's curiosity as well.

"You must truly care for your woman White Bear," he said.

"I do," answered Lazarus. "Why does that surprise you?"

"Because I have seen many red women, not just our own, but others lose their hearts to you white men," answered Chief Spotted Shield. "I have yet to see it end well."

"Many of your kind have taken our women and fathered children with them, only to abandon them," said Black Thunder.

"That's horrible," said Lazarus and he meant it. "My uncle is very much in love with his Crow wife and they just had a son. He would rather die than abandon them."

"You seem certain of this," said Chief Spotted Shield.

"I am," answered Lazarus. "He almost attacked my father for disrespecting his wife, when he was still courting her."

Black Thunder almost chuckled, but Spotted Shield was quiet and raised an eyebrow.

"When did this happen?" he asked.

"About two winters ago, when he came to visit us at my home far east of the Great River," answered Lazarus. "That is how I came out here to be a trapper."

Both Chief Spotted Shield and Black Thunder were quiet for a moment, still studying their prisoner.

"If you make it and out run my warriors tomorrow," said Black Thunder. "Will you return east to the land of your people?"

"I'm not leaving without Dark Wind," said Lazarus. "Pray that I don't make it, because if I do, I will return for her."

"Then you are a fool," said Black Thunder. "Your heart for your woman, though admirable, will only get you killed."

"If that's what it takes."

Chief Spotted Shield looked approvingly at Lazarus. He had never seen a white man like this, especially one so young.

"I believe he means what he says my son," he said in Blackfoot. "It would be unwise to underestimate him."

Black Thunder just humphed, but secretly thought that their prisoner was serious. He truly hoped that if White Bear did outrun him and his warriors tomorrow, but returned to rescue his woman, it would only give him another chance to kill him and increase his own standing among his people.

At that moment, Mountain Flower was allowed to come in and give Lazarus what was supposed to be his last meal. Neither she, nor the white youth, gave a hint of their plans. After he was done eating, he returned the bowl to her and she left the lodge followed by Chief Spotted Shield and Black Thunder.

Lazarus prayed to the Almighty that he and Dark Wind would escape from their captors. Right now it appeared that the Almighty would send an angel in the form of Mountain Flower. At least that is what Lazarus hoped.

Later that evening, when everyone was asleep, Mountain Flower managed to quietly get dressed and sneak out of Rain In The Face and Sitting Deer's lodge. Armed with a knife, she snuck around the village, to the lodge where Lazarus was held captive.

The village dogs didn't sound the alarm because they were used to her, since she had been living among them for over two years now.

She came around to the front and found the guard sleeping. Without hesitation, she quickly clamped her hand over his mouth and slit his throat.

While he lay dying, she dragged his body inside the lodge. Lazarus was awake, expecting her. She quickly cut his bonds and warned him that they have to move quickly. Using sign, Lazarus told her that he was not leaving without his wife.

She understood and told him where she was being held. They both looked out of the lodge to see if anyone sounded the alert. Suddenly, Lazarus saw Chief Spotted Shield exit his tipi to answer nature's call. He instructed Mountain Flower to get the horses, while he followed the Blackfoot leader.

Chief Spotted Shield found a bush behind his lodge. While releasing his water, a hand clamped down on his mouth.

"Don't make a sound," said Lazarus.

Spotted Shield immediately recognized the white youth's voice and also felt the knife pointed in his back. Lazarus turned him around, so he could see him face to face.

"I don't want to kill you," he said. "But if you alert your warriors, I will have no choice."

The Blackfoot Chief just nodded.

"Take me to your son's lodge."

Chief Spotted Shield led Lazarus to Black Thunder's lodge, which was right next to his. When they were in front of the lodge, Spotted Shield scratched on the lodge flap. Black Thunder was awake and surprised someone was paying him a visit at this time of night.

His father lifted the lodge flap and Lazarus gently pushed him in and followed him inside. Black Thunder, and his three wives, suddenly sat up, with their eyes wide as saucers. The children were still asleep but not for long, because Dark Wind, seeing her husband, almost shouted his name.

"Not so loud," he said. "You know why I am here Black Thunder."

Black Thunder nodded and warned his wives not to make any sudden moves. His eldest son Lightening Strikes, who appeared to be around the same age as Lazarus, was about to go for his weapons, but the trapper held his knife tight to his grandfather's throat.

"I don't want to kill your father Black Thunder," he said. "But if you don't do as I say, I will have no choice."

Black Thunder knew this was no idle threat and he ordered his son to not make any sudden movements.

"Have one of your wives release Dark Wind's bonds."

Black Thunder did as he was told and ordered one of his wives to cut Dark Wind loose. With his wife now free, Lazarus had her retrieve the weapons. Dark Wind looked outside the lodge to see if the coast was clear.

"It's safe," she said. "We can go now."

Lazarus tapped on Spotted Shield's shoulder, signaling him to back out of the lodge. Black Thunder and his family stayed frozen still, fearing for their patriarch's safety. Lazarus, Dark Wind, and Spotted Shield managed to make it to the horse herd where Mountain Flower was waiting.

Chief Spotted Shield was almost surprised to see her there. As both women mounted, Lazarus had Chief Spotted Shield's hands tied behind his back and had him sit down near a tree.

"I'm sorry it had to end like this," he said. "I didn't want to bring any harm to you and your people."

"I will be sure to tell my warriors this when they surround you and your woman," said Chief Spotted Shield. "All 200 hundred of them."

The Chief suddenly chuckled and wished White Bear and the women good luck, because they were going to need it. Lazarus immediately mounted his horse and had Mountain Flower lead the way south away from the village.

By the time Black Thunder sounded the alarm, the escaped prisoners were already riding at top speed in the night with a five-minute head start. Black Thunder and his warriors found his father tied, but unharmed. However one of the warriors reported that the guard, who was supposed to be watching White Bear, was found dead with his throat slit.

Spotted Shield told them that the Nez Perce woman, Mountain Flower, was with White Bear and his woman. With that information, they realized she was behind their prisoner's escape.

"They won't go far," said Black Thunder. "Not in the dark." "

What will we do when we catch them father?" asked Lighting Strikes.

Black Thunder looked at his own father, who just nodded. "We kill them," he finally said. "All three of them and we do it slow, so they will suffer!"

The warriors whooped in unison, all 200 hundred of them.

18

FIGHT FOR YOUR LIFE

Lazarus, Dark Wind, and Mountain Flower rode all night till the sun came up. They knew the Blackfoot would not follow them at night, but when dawn came, it would be a different story. Lazarus knew that they wouldn't be able to outrun the Blackfoot, so they needed to find higher ground and make a stand.

They had gone no more than ten miles by the time Black Thunder and his warriors left their village. They were following the Smith River when Lazarus spotted a cul de sac at the foot of the Little Belt Mountains. It wasn't much, but it was a good spot to make a stand.

"The horses won't make it any further," he said. "We need to make a stand and hold off the Blackfoot for a while."

The women agreed.

They headed to the cul de sac, where they rested the horses. Lazarus and Dark Wind prepared for the imminent attack that was coming, arming and prepping their rifles. Once Mountain Flower checked the horses she joined them, but she was only armed with a knife.

"It is best if you stay with the horses Mountain Flower," said

Lazarus in sign. "You won't be able to fight or do much with just a knife."

"The knife is for me," responded Mountain Flower. "I won't let them take me again."

Lazarus and Dark Wind looked at each other and were silent. Both knew what would happen to them if the Blackfoot caught them. Lazarus didn't believe in suicide, but he did want to be captured. As if reading her husband's thoughts, Dark Wind gently touched his hand.

"We fight together," she said. "We die together."

Lazarus just smiled. "I pray it won't come to that."

Suddenly Lazarus saw the Blackfoot coming from a distance. It was time to fight.

"Make your shots count," he said. "Here they come."

Black Thunder saw their quarry from a distance and was almost impressed that they were poised for a fight. He shouted a war cry and his warriors charged. Once they were in rifle range, Lazarus and Dark Wind fired, hitting two of the oncoming warriors. While they were in the middle of reloading, more gunfire came out of nowhere striking down more of the Blackfoot warriors. Black Thunder and his warriors stopped in mid-charge, realizing that they were being attacked from behind.

Lazarus, Dark Wind, and Mountain Flower, looked south of their position and were happy to see over a hundred Crow warriors, charging and whooping at the top of their lungs, coming straight for the Blackfoot war party.

While the Blackfeet outnumbered both the Crow war party and the trio, by more than a half, the volley of shots coming from both sides, managed to whittle down the odds a bit. Fearing that more enemy warriors were coming, Black Thunder had his men take cover, wherever they could find it.

Lazarus spotted Black Thunder and shot his horse from under him. He didn't want to kill the Blackfoot leader, not yet anyway. The Crow war party, which was led by Running Dog, Lame Deer, and

Amos Mackinnon, managed to surround the Blackfoot, firing arrows and rifles at them, and taking down many warriors.

The Blackfoot fought back valiantly, but not knowing how many Crows were attacking and taking heavy losses, most of them thought it best to retreat. Lighting Strikes managed to come to his father's aid and attempted to lift him on his horse, but Lazarus called out to Black Thunder.

"Black Thunder!!" shouted Lazarus. "I challenge you!"

The youth left the safety of the cul de sac, armed with a knife and Crow tomahawk. He approached Black Thunder and his son. This did not go unnoticed, as some of the remaining Blackfoot warriors and Crow warriors stopped fighting each other to witness what was taking place. Both Dark Wind and Amos thought Lazarus had just lost his mind, but the youth was mad and he believed that he nor his wife would have any peace while Black Thunder lived.

"Do you accept my challenge?" asked Lazarus.

"I accept," said Black Thunder.

Lighting Strikes attempted to shoot Lazarus, but his father slapped his son's gun down.

Speaking in both Blackfoot and sign, Black Thunder said," This is a fight for honor, no matter who dies, there will be no vengeance taken and the women Dark Wind and Mountain Flower are to go free."

He looked to his son as if to tell him to honor the agreement, Lighting Strikes reluctantly nodded.

Black Thunder discarded his rifle and took out his war club and knife. As they circled each other, Lazarus informed his uncle and the Crows in both Crow and sign that no matter who dies, there'll be no vengeance taken against the victor.

"Are you sure about this?" asked Uncle Amos. Not taking his eyes off of Black Thunder, Lazarus nodded.

The Crow and Blackfoot war parties surrounded the two combatants, making sure no one from either side interfered. Black Thunder was an experienced warrior, who counted many coups on many enemies. Lazarus had youth, and size on his side. However, this would be his first hand-to-hand combat and he silently prayed that this would not be his last.

Without hesitation, the two combatants charged at one another, with Black Thunder striking with his war club. Lazarus blocked it with his tomahawk and attempted to slash the warrior's midsection with his knife. Black Thunder was expecting that and managed to jump back a step, causing the youth to miss his midsection.

Black Thunder retaliated with a knife strike of his own, going for Lazarus's side, but the youth saw it coming and managed to block it with his tomahawk, however in doing so, he gave Black Thunder an opening and the warrior tried to bash Lazarus skull in with his war club.

Lazarus quickly ducked, avoiding the weapon, then without thinking, rammed his huge head into Black Thunder's midsection, knocking the wind out of the Blackfoot warrior, causing both combatants to fall to the ground, with Lazarus on top. Black Thunder lost his grip on his war club, but still had his knife and attempted to stab the trapper, but Lazarus quickly grabbed his knife arm. He stabbed at Black Thunder with his own knife, but the warrior managed to grab his knife arm.

With both men locked in arm-and-arm combat, suspense came over both the Blackfoot and Crow warriors. Amos Mackinnon and Dark Wind were both praying that Lazarus would not fall. Black Thunder was a lot stronger than Lazarus realized and was gaining the upper hand as his knife was almost to the youth's ribs.

Sensing the immediate danger, Lazarus managed to shift his weight off of Black Thunder, to keep his knife away from its intended target, but Black Thunder was crafty and he shifted his weight towards the young trapper, this time, giving him an advantage.

"Remember what your Grandda taught you," shouted Uncle Amos from the sidelines.

In a split second, Lazarus noticed that Black Thunder's groin area was unprotected, so he kicked him there hard causing the Blackfoot warrior to howl in pain and lose grip of his knife. Lazarus had his opening and managed to shift his weight back on top of the warrior and this time managed to plunge his knife into his throat. Lazarus turned the knife as the warrior's eyes widened. Black Thunder stopped moving.

For a moment there was silence. The Crows were preparing to do battle just in case the Blackfoot didn't honor their leader's word. Lazarus stood, breathing heavy, before he spoke.

"I will not take his scalp," he said. "That may be the way of most warriors here, but it is not my way."

Lazarus repeated the statement in sign and most of the Blackfoot warriors slowly nodded. Lighting Strikes approached Lazarus with hatred in eyes.

"You and your women, may leave now," he said in Blackfoot and in sign. "But know this White Bear, you have made an enemy and you will never know peace, while I draw breath."

Lazarus knew the son of Black Thunder was serious and that he truly made an enemy. But now was not the time. Enough blood had been shed that day. Dark Wind and Mountain Flower approached on horseback as Lighting Strikes took Black Thunder's body.

The Crow rescue party whooped and cheered and many individual Crow warriors, including Running Dog and Lame Deer, walked to Lazarus and patted him on the back for showing such courage. Lazarus was quiet, thinking what the young Blackfoot had said.

"I know what you're feeling lad," said Uncle Amos. "But what you just did, not only showed gumption, you have raised your station among the Crows and the Flatheads as well."

"Your Uncle is right husband," said Dark Wind. "Not only my people, but even the Blackfoot will speak of your medicine as strong."

"I didn't challenge Black Thunder to gain medicine or respect," said Lazarus.

Dark Wind would not let him finish though. "I know my husband," she said. "And I will always love you for it."

The couple embraced each other for a moment.

"We best leave," said Running Dog. "I don't trust the Blackfoot to keep their word."

"Let's go home," said Lazarus. "Oh, and thank you for coming to rescue us Running Dog, how did you know?"

"You were gone too long," said Running Dog. "Your Uncle and Plain Feather suspected that something was wrong."

Uncle Amos was staring at Mountain Flower. "Who is your friend?"

"This is Mountain Flower of the Nez Perce," answered Lazarus. "She helped Dark Wind and I escaped from the Blackfoot."

Uncle Amos approached Mountain Flower and thanked her in sign for what she did for his nephew and his wife.

"We are in your debt," he said.

"What will happen to me?" she asked in sign.

"My wife and I will return you to your people Mountain Flower," said Lazarus in sign. "You're a free woman now."

Mountain Flower was quiet for a moment.

"You will not take me?" she asked.

A confused look appeared on Lazarus's face. "Of course I will take you back to your people," he said. "I just said so."

"I don't think that's what she means husband," said Dark Wind.

Lazarus was even more confused. "I think she means do you want to take her as a second wife." Lazarus's bottom jaw suddenly dropped, while Uncle Amos and the entire Crow rescue party guffawed.

19

WHAT IS A MAN SUPPOSED TO DO?

IT WAS quiet on the way back to the Bighorn River. It took a couple of days to get back to the village of Medicine Hawk, but no one was in a rush. While some of the warriors hunted for the group, Lazarus was in deep thought about Mountain Flower.

While she was a very beautiful woman, the very thought of taking her as a second wife, horrified him. He felt like it would be a slap in the face to Dark Wind. What shocked him even more was that Dark Wind had said very little about the situation and didn't appear to be remotely angry with him or Mountain Flower.

The two women had been conversing with each other since they left Blackfoot country, but they were very quiet about it. Lazarus looked at his uncle, who would often grin in amusement at his nephew. Lazarus wasn't expecting any help this time from him.

"How the hell did I get myself into this?" he thought to himself.

They arrived back at the Crow village to much fanfare and to the relief of friends and relatives. Uncle Amos was greeted with a huge hug and kiss from Plain Feather and he reciprocated in kind, before taking their infant son and holding him up high while beaming with pride.

It was great to be home. Chief Medicine Hawk and his family as well as the council were relieved that Lazarus and Dark Wind were alright, and after Running Dog and Amos explained the situation and told how Lazarus challenged and killed the Blackfoot warrior Black Thunder there were gasps, followed by cheers and whoops.

"I have heard of this Black Thunder," said Medicine Hawk. "To defeat such an enemy one-on-one is no small thing."

The Crow leader placed his hands on the young trapper's shoulders and beamed with pride.

"You have brought great honor to your family White Bear," he said. "Not only will the Crow praise your medicine, but your wife's people the Flathead as well."

"We should hold a feast in his honor," said Red Star, who was the Holy Man of the village.

"The honor is not mine alone," said Lazarus in both Crow and sign. The young trapper gently took Mountain Flower by the hand and introduced her to everyone. "If it wasn't for Mountain Flower, my wife and I never would have been able to escape from the Blackfoot,"

Lazarus explained how the Nez Perce woman was taken from her people by none other than Snake In The Grass and she was a slave among them for almost two summers.

"Dark Wind and I would not be standing before you now if it wasn't for Mountain Flower," said Lazarus. "She killed to help free us and she deserves just as much honor and respect as me or my uncle or any of the Crow warriors who came to our rescue."

No one disagreed with Lazarus's statement. Running Dog, Lame Deer, and Dark Wind concurred and added that the Nez Perce woman had strong medicine, despite all that she had suffered. Mountain Flower was quiet but she was appreciative of what the trapper known as White Bear and his Flathead woman and their Crow friends were saying about her. Amos whispered something into Plain Feather's ear, which caused his bride to chuckle.

"Something amusing White Horse Talker?" asked Chief Medicine Hawk.

"I was just telling your daughter here, that Mountain Flower would make a fine second wife to my nephew," answered Uncle Amos.

Lazarus nearly popped a blood vessel. "Uncle Amos, are you trying to get me killed?!!"

Everyone was looking at Lazarus in confusion. "My Uncle White Horse Talker is only joking," he said in Crow and sign. "I have no intention of taking Mountain Flower or any other woman as a second wife."

"Why not, Lazarus?" asked Dark Wind.

Lazarus looked at his bride in horror. He then looked at the crowd and saw some looks of confusion, but mostly looks of amusement, including Chief Medicine Hawk, Running Dog, and Lame Deer. When he turned to his Uncle Amos, the latter just shrugged.

"Don't look at me nephew," said Uncle Amos. "Your wife is the one asking the question."

"You're no help," said Lazarus. "Thanks for nothing."

"My pleasure," responded Uncle Amos with a chuckle.

Lazarus turned to his wife and looked deeply into her eyes. "I can't take her as a second wife," he said. "Even if I wanted to."

"Why?"

"For one, it is because I love you, Dark Wind," answered Lazarus. "The mere thought of taking another woman, to me is an act of betrayal and after all that we have been through I could never do that to you. Hear me, Never!"

Plain Feather and Uncle Amos were just standing there listening in awe of their nephew.

"You sure he is not your son, instead of your nephew, husband?" asked Plain Feather jokingly. "I mean he does look like you and he acts like you."

"That's disgusting," responded Amos. "That is my sister's son you're talking about."

Mountain Flower, who didn't speak or understand English, was just standing and listening to the conversation between White Bear and Dark Wind. While she couldn't understand it, she knew that they were talking about her.

Dark Wind, after hearing the loving words from her husband stating that his heart belongs to her and her alone, melted her own heart and a tear came down her cheek. Lazarus gently wiped it away as he continued to explain to her why he wouldn't take a second wife.

"Among my people," He said. "Men don't take second or third wives, not while they are still married to the first one."

"Truly?" asked Dark Wind.

Lazarus nodded. "At least they are not supposed to, not while the first one is still living."

"I'm learning more about you white men every day," said Plain Feather. "And I am happily married to one."

"You should have told her Uncle Amos," said Lazarus.

"This is about you and the situation you got yourself into, nephew," responded Uncle Amos. "This isn't about me."

"Relax White Bear," said Plain Feather. "Your Uncle has no intention of taking a second wife, are you husband?"

Uncle Amos just winked. "I have a better chance of jumping off a cliff and landing into a grizzly bear's den and living to tell the tale."

Dark Wind thought that she, Lazarus, and Mountain Flower needed privacy, so she took both of them by the hand and guided them back to the lodge that she and Lazarus shared. Amos, Plain Feather and the rest of the village looked on in amusement.

"Lazarus," she said. "Your words make me happy and proud to be your woman."

Lazarus sensed a but coming on.

"Just as you have given your heart to me, mine will always be yours," said Dark Wind. "But Mountain Flower has no one."

"What about her people?" asked Lazarus. "Surely she still has family there."

"Snake In The Grass killed her father and the man she was supposed to marry," said Dark Wind. "While his parents were kind to her, he was not."

Dark Wind didn't need to explain what Snake In The Grass had done to Mountain Flower.

"She told you this?"

Dark Wind nodded. "Among my people, and hers, men of great standing are known to have more than one wife. Especially if they can take care of them."

"Is this what you want?"

"I don't believe it matters what I want, it matters what is right for us and for her," said Dark Wind. "Think of it this way, I could be with child and we can use the help, not to mention an extra hand with the hunting and the trapping would be beneficial."

"I haven't thought of that," said Lazarus.

It was quiet for a moment, Lazarus felt that he was between a rock and a hard place. He loved Dark Wind and she knew it. She loved him even more and the fact that he would not do anything that was considered dishonorable made her even more proud to be his wife.

Before he made his decision, Lazarus turned to Mountain Flower. "Mountain Flower," he said in sign. "Do you wish to be my wife?"

Mountain Flower looked at Dark Wind, who smiled in return. For the first time since she met both of them, the Nez Perce woman gave a slight smile, before she nodded.

"I don't have much," said Lazarus in sign. "But I promise you this, you will be loved, respected, and protected by not just me and Dark Wind, but by my Uncle and his family as well."

Lazarus paused for a moment to make sure she understood.

"You are family now and you will be treated as such," he said. "I cannot imagine what you have suffered, but I promise you this, no man or woman will ever force themself on you or hold you against your will ever again. I will pledge my life to you and Dark Wind as a man should."

Mountain Flower looked deep into the young trapper's eyes and believed every word he said.

"Thank you," she said in sign.

After that she hugged Lazarus, crying hysterically. Lazarus just held her in comfort, as she continued to weep. After hearing what Snake In The Grass put her through, Lazarus was now glad that he killed him in battle.

"Son of bitch got off too easy," He said to himself.

He let go of Mountain Flower for a moment and turned to Dark Wind.

"Stay here with her," he said. "I will go tell everyone the good news."

Dark Wind smiled and immediately kissed her husband. It lasted a while, much to their pleasure, before they reluctantly released each other and Lazarus exited the lodge. After he left, Dark Wind sat next to Mountain Flower.

"He meant every word he said," she said in sign.

"I believe him," said Mountain Flower in sign. "You are blessed to have him for a husband."

"As are you now," said Dark Wind. "My sister."

Mountain Flower smiled as tears of joy streamed down her cheeks. Without hesitation, Dark Wind hugged her and let her know that all was well.

20

SUMMER OF 1812

With summer around the corner, Lazarus and Uncle Amos continued to trap the Bighorn River. They brought in loads of beaver. During that time, everyone got the chance to know Mountain Flower better.

She was just a year younger than both Lazarus and Dark Wind. She was allowed to mourn the death of her father and betrothed at the hands of Snake In The Grass but she never fully recovered. Especially after the his repeated violation of her.

Many a night she would wake up screaming and end up in tears. Lazarus and Dark Wind would comfort her, letting her know that her suffering had ended. Lazarus would sometimes sing a Scottish tune in Gaelic, that his grandfather would sing to him and his sister when they were still babies.

It had the intended effect. Before long Mountain Flower's nightmares would disappear, especially after Dark Wind showed her the scalp of Snake In The Grass. Together they would both put a curse on it, praying to the Creator that his spirit would suffer as it wandered this life never being able to enter the Happy Hunting Grounds.

Lazarus was often curious about the religious beliefs of the Crow, Flathead, and Nez Perce tribes, or any tribes he came in contact with.

Despite growing up in his family's Presbyterian faith, he was not religious. He believed in the Bible and Jesus Christ, but he was more
spiritual.

However, at the same time he didn't disavow the beliefs of the
American Indian tribes. Uncle Amos was the same way and
explained to his nephew that each tribe has a different belief system,
but it was more like a way of life than a religion.

That's what made living among the Crow and Flathead easier for
both Uncle and nephew, accepting what they had in common with
the tribes more than what made them different. Lazarus often
thought about his family back in Delaware and how they were doing.

He thought mostly about his grandda and how much he missed
him. He didn't have a bad childhood, far from it. However, he didn't
enjoy the strict religious upbringing that his parents instilled in him
and his siblings. GrandDa Mackinnon made things not only a little
easier but more fun, especially since he taught his grandchildren how
to fight and never back down from bullies.

The lessons that his grandfather taught him helped Lazarus
much, especially when it came to one-on-one combat fighting. While
Lazarus never went looking for trouble, he was the last person to
back down from it. Especially when it came to protecting the ones he
loved.

While most whites, especially those claiming to be Christians,
looked down on Indians as nothing more than godless heathens who
needed to be either wiped out or removed from their homelands,
both Uncle Amos and Lazarus saw it much differently.

It was because of this issue that uncle and nephew, decided that
they would never move back east though they missed their kin.
However both Plain Feather and Dark Wind were very interested in
wanting to know much about their husbands' kin back east and, if
the opportunity ever came up, they even mentioned traveling back
east to visit. As they were packing up their plews to head downriver to
St. Louis to trade,

it was Dark Wind who brought it up.

"Do you ever think about your family back home?" she asked Lazarus.

"From time to time," he said.

Mountain Flower had been learning English, Flathead, and some Crow, so she was able to understand what was being said. She too was interested in Lazarus and Amos' relatives.

"You rarely speak about them," she said in heavily accented English.

"Not much to say," said Lazarus. "Uncle Amos, Aunt Plain Feather, White Cloud and you two lovely ladies are my family now."

Both women beamed at him for that statement. Uncle Amos and Aunt Plain Feather had been listening and were curious.

"Why do you ladies ask?" asked Uncle Amos.

Both women just shrugged. "I hope to one day meet the family I owe my happiness to," said Dark Wind.

"I have felt the same way," said Plain Feather all of a sudden. "Our son should know something of his father's world."

A look of sadness appeared on Uncle Amos's face.

"I'm afraid all of you would be disappointed," he said.

"You believe your family would not accept us," said Dark Wind.

It was a statement, not a question.

"I know they wouldn't," said Lazarus. "Especially my mother."

"Make no mistake ladies," said Uncle Amos. "We have no regrets in taking you for our wives and we would love nothing more than to take you back to Delaware and have you meet our kin."

"But you're afraid of how we will be treated," said Plain Feather.

Uncle Amos nodded. "I will kill to protect you and our son," he said. "You know this."

"He means it Aunt Plain Feather," said Lazarus with a grin. "He threatened to kill my father when he found out that you were not white."

"I wasn't going to kill him, Lazarus," said Amos. "Just warned him to choose his next words carefully."

"Then you would have killed him?"

"Bloody Hell No!!" said Amos. "Just mess him up a bit. I mean, after all, he is still your Da and my sister's husband."

Lazarus just chuckled. "I love my parents and brothers too, but if they said anything against Dark Wind and Mountain Flower I probably would do more than mess them up a bit."

"You shouldn't talk like that husband," said Dark Wind. "They are still your blood."

"Yes, dear."

"We shouldn't worry about it, because it will never happen," said Uncle Amos.

"And what gives you such confidence, husband?" asked Plain Feather.

"For one, Delaware is too far, it would take months to get there and back," said Uncle Amos. "And two, once we visit St. Louis and sell our plews you wouldn't want to go any further than there."

"It would still be nice to meet your family," said Dark Wind. "Especially your Grandfather, I'm sure he would love to meet his great-grandchild."

"Great-Grandchild?" said Lazarus all of sudden. Then it hit him, as Dark Wind smiled.

"We're going to have a baby?"

"Next winter," said Dark Wind. "On the moon, you whites call January."

"Yahooo!!!!" shouted Lazarus as he picked up Dark Wind and danced a jig. Uncle Amos, Aunt Plain Feather and Mountain Flower, all laughed at the antics of the proud parents-to-be.

They left the village of Chief Medicine Hawk that morning. Traveling twenty miles a day and hunting while resting, they made good time. They arrived at Fort Lisa, the first week of June. There they met Toussaint Charbonneau and his wife the famed Shoshone guide, Sacagawea.

Meeting the famous couple from the Corps Of Discovery was the highlight of the trip. Manuel Lisa offered to buy Amos and Lazarus' plews, but they respectfully declined, knowing that they could get better prices in St. Louis.

Manuel Lisa warned them to be careful because there had been whispers of war with the British. The group took the warning seriously and left Fort Lisa a couple of days later, following the Missouri River. They arrived in St. Louis at the end of June, where they found out that Lisa's warning about the War with Britain was no whisper but fact. A chance run-in with Amos and Lazarus's old friend John Colter, confirmed it.

On June 18, 1812, the United States declared war with Great Britain in what would be known as the War Of 1812. While St. Louis was not entirely affected by it, the surrounding areas: Illinois, Ohio, Kentucky and the rest of the Missouri Territory were. Loyalties between tribes and neighbors were tested. Both Uncle Amos and Lazarus were concerned, mainly because of how it could affect the Fur Trade.

"We best sell our plews, resupply ourselves, and head back west quickly," said Uncle Amos.

No one disagreed. They met Manuel Lisa's partner Jean-Pierre Chouteau, whose son Auguste P. Chouteau had bought plews from Amos and Lazarus last year. This time Amos and Lazarus had brought in 1,022 beaver plews and, after the elder Chouteau found them to be in prime condition, like his son did last summer, he bought each plew for a generous price of $10 a plew; making both uncle and nephew very rich men.

They resupplied themselves for the next two trapping seasons while visiting John Colter for a couple of days. The former mountain man, and his wife Sally, were the proud parents of a healthy boy named Hiram. Lazarus informed John that he and Dark Wind were expecting and they were congratulated. Colter also congratulated Lazarus on having two wives after the youth explained how he accomplished that feat.

"I always knew the lad had it in him," joked Uncle Amos.

"I somehow knew that too," said Colter. "You two ladies take good care of him and that goes double for you Plain Feather, Amos needs a good woman to keep him grounded."

"I agree," said Plain Feather.

After saying goodbye to their friend and his family, Uncle Amos and Lazarus deposited the rest of their money in their bank accounts. While they had no intention of living in St. Louis anytime soon, a man never knew when and if he would need money. Though it was useless on the frontier.

They left St. Louis the second week of July, following the Missouri River north. They avoided human contact, both white and red, until they found themselves in Omaha country and were greeted by Yellow Bull and his people.

They spent a couple of days with the Omaha, trading and hunting, before continuing their journey home to the Crow Village of Chief Medicine Hawk. They were going to spend the rest of the summer there, before heading to the Flathead Village of Snake Killer on the Clark Fork River, where they will spend the winter.

21

LIGHTING STRIKES REVENGE

AFTER SPENDING the rest of the summer with the Crow, Lazarus, Amos and his wives traveled to Flathead country. They went to their usual trapping spot near Silver Bow Creek, close to the Clark Fork River. While there, they began settling down and decided to make a permanent home.

While they continued to live in teepees, the Uncle and nephew duo built a smoke house to dry meat. They built a dugout as well. They sheltered some of the animals in the dugout and planned on building cabins in the spring.

The women had never seen a cabin, however, Plain Feather had heard of them before. Her people called them wood lodges and found it unusual that her husband and nephew would suggest living in one all year round. They thought that a teepee that you can build up and take down as you travel was more practical.

Both Amos and Lazarus assured the women that living in a cabin would be better than living in a teepee. They asked the women to give it a try for at least a year, if they didn't like it, then they can move and live anywhere else or live the way their people have lived for generations.

The women agreed, because they knew the men were true to

their word. Another promise Lazarus planned on keeping was taking Mountain Flower back to her people, to let them know that she was alive. While she was free to leave anytime she wished, she chose to stay with the trapper known as White Bear as his second wife.

Both Lazarus and Dark Wind had been a huge comfort for her and, while she was happy that they were going to have a baby, she wanted one of her own and she wanted it to be Lazarus's baby. She enjoyed babysitting Angus White Cloud, who was now a year old and was getting bigger and stronger everyday.

His parents treated Mountain Flower like a daughter, despite that Plain Feather wasn't that much older. Though she was very mature for her age and she and Amos had a strong bond in their marriage. While most marriages between trappers and Indian women were based on necessity, Amos and Plain Feather's marriage was truly based on love. Before long, Lazarus grew to love Mountain Flower.

As the winter trapping season began, Amos and Lazarus trapped the Clark Fork River and brought many beaver pelts as they did previous seasons. During the beginning of October, they were happily visited by none other than Dark Wind's brother Lone Falcon and their cousin Shooting Arrow.

They brought the two Flathead warriors into their camp and Lone Falcon was overjoyed to see that he was going to be an uncle. Dark Wind was showing, and both she and Lazarus were excited about the upcoming birth. They introduced Mountain Flower to Lone Falcon and Shooting Arrow, explaining how she became Lazarus's second wife. They listened attentively about how she helped him and Dark Wind escape the Blackfoot earlier that spring.

After hearing this, both men welcomed her into their family. They stayed the night, before inviting the entire group to the village, which was not far from the camp. It was a joyous reunion in the village of Snake Killer. Plenty Hawk and Fighting Bear Woman were excited that they were going to have a grandchild soon and, after meeting Mountain Flower and hearing her story, she was welcomed into the family and a feast was held in her honor.

They spent most of the winter in Snake Killer's village, going out mostly to hunt and trap. As the winter of 1812 turned into 1813, Lazarus celebrated his nineteenth birthday. A week later on January 11, Dark Wind gave birth to a healthy baby boy.

Lazarus and Amos were hunting for meat to help provide for the village at the time and managed to bring down a bull moose despite the harsh winter. They brought it back to the village just in time to hear the good news that Lazarus was a father. He was allowed to go in and see his wife and son and gently held the baby for the first time.

"He looks like my Grand Da," he said.

The baby had light skin, but small jet black hair, like an Indian. However, his eyes were blue like his father's and he had his father's nose. Today was a happy day. Amos and Plenty Hawk came inside the lodge where Dark Wind was surrounded by her mother, Mountain Flower, Lone Falcon's wife Red Calf, and Plain Feather.

"What do you wish to name your son?" asked Dark Wind.

Lazarus paused for a moment and beamed at his Uncle Amos. " His name shall be Amos," he said.

"You sure you want to do that to the lad?" laughed Uncle Amos.

"I think it is a great name," said Plain Feather.

Their son Angus White Cloud walked to his big cousin and the latter held the baby out to him. The little tyke gave his new baby cousin a peck on his forehead and giggled.

"He must have a Flathead name," said Lazarus. "Any candidates?"

"Winter Hawk," said Dark Wind. Lazarus thought for a moment.

"Amos Winter Hawk Buchanan," he said. "I like it!"

"It is a good name," said Plenty Hawk.

Lazarus handed the baby to his grandfather, who gently held him up high and thanked the Creator for this little miracle in the midst of winter.

As Winter turned into Spring, Uncle Amos and Lazarus began searching for new trapping grounds. Since Lazarus and Dark Wind both had planned on taking Mountain Flower to see her people, and her people lived over the Continental Divide, they thought that they could kill two birds with one stone. Lazarus brought the idea to Uncle

Amos while they were hunting with Plenty Hawk and Lone Falcon one day.

"Mountain Flower told me that her people live over the Divide," he said. "Where we met Andrew Henry and his men two years ago?"

"Around there yeah," said Uncle Amos.

Then he stopped and looked around. The trees seemed to be still in the gentle breeze. Too quiet. Lazarus instinctively kept his mouth shut as he, his uncle, father-in-law and brother-in-law scan the woods. Something or someone was in the area. Suddenly Uncle Amos shouted.

"Lazarus lookout!!" Uncle Amos quickly shoved his nephew out of the way as a long Blackfoot lance hurled in his direction.

However, as Amos pushed his nephew out of harm's way, he put himself into it, the lance impaled itself into his abdomen.

"No!!!!!" cried Lazarus.

"Blackfoot," shouted Plenty Hawk.

But it wasn't a war party, it was only one Blackfoot and it was none other than Lighting Strikes, the son of Black Thunder, who Lazarus killed in a fair one on one fight last spring.

Lazarus looked up at the lone warrior, whose face was painted and smiling, as if issuing a challenge to the trapper. Lazarus knew why he was there and he was happy to oblige the enemy. Lone Falcon was about to fire his rifle at Lighting Strikes, but Lazarus quickly slapped it down.

"He's mine," said Lazarus with venom.

Lighting Strikes disappeared into the woods, willfully leaving a trail. Lazarus grabbed his Pennsylvania rifle, checked his weapons and followed.

"Get my uncle to the village," he said in Flathead. "I will finish this."

"It could be a trap," said Lone Falcon.

Amos was still alive, but was coughing up blood. "Be careful Lazarus," he said. "You finish that bastard and bring back his scalp!"

"Don't you worry about that, Uncle."

Lazarus followed the retreating Lighting Strikes into the thick underbrush while Plenty Hawk and Lone Falcon attended to Uncle Amos. The Blackfoot warrior left a trail in which the youth cautiously followed. He thought this could be a trap, but he didn't care.

He should have known that, after defeating Black Thunder last year, his son would want revenge. He came into an opening and saw Lighting Strikes alone, armed with a knife and a war club. It was the same war club that belonged to his father.

It was clear that the warrior was issuing a challenge and Lazarus accepted. He discarded his rifle and pistols and took out his Crow tomahawk and Arkansas toothpick. Lazarus didn't ask if Lightning Strikes was alone. He didn't need to.

He immediately shouted out a war cry and charged. Lightning Strikes charged as well and before they knew it, they were entangled in battle. The Blackfoot warrior struck with his war club, but Lazarus ducked and struck with his tomahawk, hitting the Blackfoot's arm that carried his war club.

The fight was quick and brutal, as Lazarus struck again with his tomahawk. Lightning Strikes dodged it, protecting his wounded arm. He quickly dropped his knife and tossed his war club into his knife hand and tried to strike again with his father's weapon.

Lazarus was one step ahead, blocked Lightning Strikes war club strike with his tomahawk and at the same time managed to strike the Blackfoot warrior's midsection with his knife, opening a deep slash and exposing his intestines.

Lightning Strikes fell to his knees in shock, dropping his war club and trying to hold in his organs. Lazarus stood before him, with pure rage in his eyes. Lightning Strikes sang singing his death song and, without hesitation, Lazarus buried his tomahawk into his enemy's skull killing him instantly. It was over.

22

MAN OF THE MOUNTAIN

LAZARUS TOOK LIGHTING STRIKES' scalp and left his body to the elements. He was on his way back to the village when Plenty Hawk and his warriors arrived.

"Are you hurt my son?" asked Plenty Hawk.

Lazarus shook his head. When asked about Lightning Strikes, Lazarus just raised his scalp.

"He won't be a problem any more."

"This is good," said Plenty Hawk. "But you must hurry."

"Uncle Amos?"

"He doesn't have much time."

Lone Falcon rode up with Lazarus's horse. The youth quickly mounted and rode back to the village with his friends.

Amos MacKinnon didn't have much time left on earth. He was surrounded by his wife, their infant son, and friends from the village. The Medicine Man Black Cloud did what he could, but the trapper had lost too much blood. It was only a matter of time.

Lazarus stopped his horse in front of his uncle's lodge. He was quickly guided in by his wives. They didn't need to tell him the grim news. Amos looked up at his nephew and smiled.

"Is it finished?" he asked.

Lazarus showed his uncle Lighting Strikes' scalp.

"It is done uncle," he said. "Now all you need to worry about is getting better."

"I'm afraid it is too late nephew," responded Uncle Amos. "My time on earth is ending."

"Don't say that!" shouted Lazarus. "You can't die, you have a son to raise and there is still so much to do!"

"I'm afraid I don't have a say in the matter, nephew," said Uncle Amos. "But do not grieve. I have lived a good life and long enough to be proud of the man that you have become."

Lazarus immediately broke down crying as he held his uncle's hand. Amos had been more like a father than an uncle and he'd kept his promise to Lazarus' parents that he would watch out for him.

"There is nothing left to teach, nothing to be ashamed of," he said while coughing up blood. "You're a man now, a man of the mountain, who answers to no one but God and himself."

"I don't know how to go on without you Uncle Amos," said Lazarus.

"You can and you will," said Uncle Amos. "You're stronger than you know, just promise me one thing."

"Anything!"

"Look after your Aunt Plain Feather and your cousin Angus for me," said Uncle Amos. "At least until she has finished her time of mourning, then allow her to remarry."

"I promise," said Lazarus. "Don't forget you have your own family to look after now, and don't forget your promise to Mountain Flower to return her to her people."

Uncle Amos looked at Dark Wind and Mountain Flower and smiled at them as he nodded, before turning to Plain Feather.

"I wish we had more time together, my love," he said. "I pray I was a good husband to you."

"A very good husband," said Plain Feather as tears flowed down her cheeks.

Angus White Cloud cried as his mother sat him before his father. Uncle Amos gently touched the boy's cheek wiping away the tears.

"Remember me, my son," he said in Crow. "Father, I'm ready to come home."

Those were Amos MacKinnon's last words. He breathed his last. Lazarus bowed his head, crying, as the women wailed in unison. With the death of Amos MacKinnon it was the end of an era, while a new one began with his nephew Lazarus Buchanan.

The next day Amos' body was taken to the spot near Silver Bow Creek where he and his nephew were going to build a couple of cabins. He was buried not nearby in a Flathead funeral. While he never mentioned much about his religious beliefs, among his personal belongings was a King James Bible.

Remembering his Presbyterian upbringing, Lazarus opened his Uncle's bible and read from Psalms 23:1-6. They sent word to the Crow village of Medicine Hawk and a week later, the entire village came to Silver Bow Creek to pay their respect. He was remembered as a great warrior and an honorable man, a great friend.

During the rest of the Spring of 1813, Lazarus and the women built two cabins. One for all of them to share and one to store their beaver pelts. True to his word, Lazarus looked after his Aunt Plain Feather and cousin Angus White Cloud, who along with Lazarus' own son, Amos Winterhawk, continued to grow healthy and strong.

Every morning when he would go hunting or trapping, Lazarus would stop by his uncle's grave to pay his respects. It had been very hard on him, even though months had passed since his death. One evening after dinner, Plain Feather took him outside to talk to him.

"It's not your fault, nephew," she said.

"It should have been me."

"But it wasn't," she countered. "Your Uncle sacrificed his life to save yours as you would have done the same for him."

Lazarus was quiet. He understood why his uncle took Plain Feather as his wife, for she was full of wisdom like him.

"I miss him too," she said. "But we must live on as he would have wanted it."

"I understand," said Lazarus. "He kept his promise to me Mum and Grand Da, that he would look out for me."

"Then don't let it be in vain," said Plain Feather. "You're a man now, a Man of The Mountains."

EPILOGUE

May of 1822, Silver Bow Creek, Montana

As LAZARUS and Amos Winterhawk finished packing the animals for the journey east to sell their plews, Dark Wind and Mountain Flower had finished checking the cabin, making sure that everything was clean and tidy before closing the door and securing it shut.

The family would be gone for possibly the entire summer and a lot can happen in the mountains. They were planning on stopping by the Crow village of Medicine Hawk to visit Aunt Plain Feather and cousin Amos White Cloud.

Since Uncle Amos' death, Plain Feather has since remarried to a good man, who had taken and raised young Amos White Cloud as his own son. However, keeping the promise to the boy's father, Lazarus would often tell wonderful stories about his Uncle Amos to his cousin.

Lazarus, Plain Feather, and even Dark Wind and Mountain Flower, made sure that the boy would never forget who his father was and that he was a good man. Lazarus himself had become a devoted family to his two wives and three sons, raising them in the dangerous, unpredictable, frontier of America.

It was not easy, but by Divine Providence and help from friends such as the Flathead, Crow, and Nez Perce, Lazarus Buchanan known as White Bear managed to beat the odds. He dodged the fate of those others who come to the frontier and end up never being heard from again, bodies bleached by the face of the sun.

AUTHOR'S NOTE

It should be noted that the main reason the Blackfoot, who were the Lords of the Northern Plains, were so hostile to the American Fur Trappers, is because of two things. One, in 1806, when Meriweather Lewis and two companions from the Corps Of Discovery murdered two Blackfoot teenagers at the Two Medicine River, and two, the beaver was considered sacred to the Blackfoot people and their way of life. For the trappers to come into their territory without permission and basically killing and slaugthering the beaver was considered sacrilege. It would be the equivalent of someone burning a Christian church or Catholic Cathedral. The fact that after two near death experiences with the Blackfoot at Three Forks, Montana, John Colter would have learned his lesson and to a point he did, when he warned Manuel Lisa and Andrew Henry that to go to Three Forks to trade with the Blackfoot and trap beaver was foolish and suicide. However, thinking safety in numbers, he was convinced to guide Andrew Henry and his men to Three Forks. That turned out to be a mistake. A fatal mistake for some of Andrew Henry's men, like George Drouillard, but a final mistake for John Colter who basically had enough and left Three Forks and the frontier for the final time at the beginning of April 1810. He arrived in St. Louis at the beginning of May, where would marry a woman named Sallie and they would have a son, Hiram. After all that however, John Colter would die from jaundice on November 22, 1813 and is buried in what is now New Haven, Missouri.

The place and timeline where I have Andrew Henry and his men crossing the Continental Divide into Idaho and built Fort Henry, from 1810-1811 is pretty much accurate. Andrew Henry left Fort Manuel on the Three Forks, not long after the death of George Drouillard, due to the many attacks from the Blackfoot. While he and sixty men did manage to trap some beaver on Henry's Fork, it wasn't enough to make a fortune for the Missouri Fur Company as he had hoped. In fact, the first three years of the Missouri Fur Company was considered unprofitable, causing it to be reorganized four or five times, until its dissolution in 1830.

While this book is a work of fiction, I have done my best to make it historically accurate. It is the first book in my new series and I hope that you have enjoyed reading it, as much as I have enjoyed writing it. I would like to thank all my readers, friends and family; along with Nick Wale, Katrina Achey, Kevin and Misty Diamond, and the entire Dusty Saddle Publishing crew for their love and support. Aho!

ABOUT THE AUTHOR

LeRoy A. Peters is an Air Force veteran and graduate of Montana State University in Bozeman,
MT. He is a published author of the Edge Of The World Trilogy and Saga Of The Armstrong Brothers series and has published a stand alone novel entitled Where The Wind Takes You. He is a huge fan of authors who have written novels set in the Fur Trade, such as the late Win Blevins, the late Richard S. Wheeler, Lane R.Warenski, David Robbins, D.L. Bittick, Porter Mills III, John Legg, M. Wayne Zillman, Robert M. Johnson, W. Michael Gear and the late Terry C. Johnston. He is a strong advocate for American Indian rights and has read books of famous American Indian heroes such as Sitting Bull, Gall, Crazy Horse, Geronimo, Black Kettle, Logan Fontenelle, Quanah Parker and in recent times Dennis Banks. A native of Clarksville, Maryland, he currently resides in Newark

Made in the USA
Columbia, SC
24 August 2024

41115519R00078